"You're good with the girls."

The compliment sent heat crawling toward her cheeks.

She hadn't forgotten Connor was still in the room with her. She just hadn't realized he'd turned around and was now watching her closely. *Intently.*

What did he see on her face? Longing? Regret? Her wish to do things differently this time around?

Olivia glanced up, hearing the gratitude in his voice. Their eyes met across the short distance between them.

At this close range she could see every nuance of color in his golden eyes, and every unfiltered emotion, a few she didn't recognize or understand. "I can't think of anything I'd rather do than watch your girls this summer."

"I can't think of anyone I'd rather watch them."

He didn't smile as he said the words, yet something pleasant shifted between them, something that went beyond words, something Olivia couldn't quite define.

Maybe she wasn't supposed to try. At least not right now.

Books by Renee Ryan

Love Inspired

  Homecoming Hero
  †*Claiming the Doctor's Heart*

Love Inspired Historical

*The Marshal Takes a Bride
*Hannah's Beau
  Heartland Wedding
*Loving Bella
  Dangerous Allies
*The Lawman Claims His Bride
  Courting the Enemy
  Mistaken Bride
*Charity House Courtship

*The Outlaw's Redemption
*Finally a Bride

*Charity House
†Village Green

To browse a current listing of all Renee's titles, please visit www.Harlequin.com.

RENEE RYAN

grew up in a small Florida beach town. To entertain herself during countless hours of "lying out," she read all the classics. It wasn't until the summer between her sophomore and junior years at Florida State University that she read her first romance novel. Hooked from page one, she spent hours consuming one book after another while working on the best (and last!) tan of her life.

Two years later, armed with a degree in economics and religion, she explored various career opportunities, including stints at a Florida theme park, a modeling agency and a cosmetics conglomerate. She moved on to teach high school while coaching award-winning cheerleading teams. Several years later, with an eclectic cast of characters swimming around in her head, she began seriously pursuing a writing career. Renee lives in Nebraska with her husband and an ornery cat. Visit her online at www.reneeryan.com.

Claiming the Doctor's Heart

Renee Ryan

Recycling programs for this product may not exist in your area.

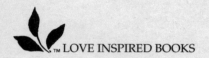

™ LOVE INSPIRED BOOKS

ISBN-13: 978-0-373-81759-7

CLAIMING THE DOCTOR'S HEART

Printed in U.S.A.

In his heart a man plans his course,
but the Lord determines his steps.
—*Proverbs* 16:9

To my fabulous husband, Mark.
Not only for inspiring Connor,
both in character and looks, but for being with me
every step of the way this time around.
I seriously couldn't have finished this book without you.
I love you with all my heart.

Chapter One

Make a plan. Work the plan. Adjust when necessary.

Olivia Scott had rescued countless companies from financial ruin with that particular strategy. Why not use the same winning formula in her own life?

No more excuses. No more waiting for the perfect moment to come along. With only six months before she turned the Big 3-0, and nothing tying her to her old life, this was her chance to strike out on her own.

"If not now, when?"

Her bold words echoed in the empty kitchen of her childhood home, disappearing beneath the hum of the refrigerator.

Olivia squared her shoulders, refusing to allow any more darkness in her heart this morning. Losing her job didn't have to be a bad thing. Nor did she have to regret finding out her ex-boyfriend only thought of her as a convenience. Better to know before she agreed to marry him, instead of after.

Olivia dropped her forehead to the kitchen table, squeezed her eyes shut and drew in several long, calming breaths.

Moving back to Colorado from Jacksonville, Florida, could be a blessing in disguise. The very nudge she needed to stop dreaming about opening her own tearoom and start making it happen.

Step one: make a plan.

Olivia lifted her head, turned on her laptop and looked around the kitchen while the machine booted up. Nothing had changed. The white enameled sink still had the long crack in the middle. The golden handles on the dark cabinets were original, as was the terra-cotta tile floor at her feet. This had been her mother's domain, where she'd taught Olivia natural ingredients were always the best.

She really missed her mother.

Sighing, Olivia turned her attention back to the computer screen, clicked on the Village Green's Chamber of Commerce official website and scrolled through the registry of businesses.

Some were new. Most had been around for generations.

She clicked on the link to a chocolate shop, frowned when she saw it had gone out of business six months ago and sat back in her chair. Wasn't that interesting?

She returned to the search engine, typed in the words *Colorado* and *Chocolatier* and—

A wet nose nudged her hand.

Looking down, she steeled her heart against large, pleading brown eyes. "No, Baloo, I can't go for a walk right now."

Leash clamped between his teeth, her brother's ancient black Lab shivered from head to toe. "No, really, I can't. Maybe later, I'll…"

Well, why not?

What better way to organize the ideas swirling around in her head? It wouldn't hurt to avoid her two brothers, either, or their questions concerning her sudden arrival last night.

Losing her job had only been the first painful loss she'd endured before coming home. She hadn't planned to bunk in her childhood bed, in the house she and her brothers had inherited when their parents died in a car crash ten years ago. Yet here she was.

A canine whine pulled her thoughts back to the present. Olivia made a face at the fifty-pound dog. "I'm not fooled, you know. I just let you out a half hour ago."

The dog danced sideways to the back door, gave a pitiful swish of his tail, then pawed at the wood.

"All right, O impatient one." Olivia drew the leash from his mouth and snapped it into his collar. "Let's go."

Once outside, instead of heading toward Main Street, she turned south. She wasn't in a talkative mood. The fewer people she ran into this morning, the better.

It was an idyllic summer morning, in a small town straight out of a 1950s television show. Flowers bloomed in the tidy lawns along the lane. Birdsong filled the air. In the near distance, the majestic Rocky Mountains punched their craggy peaks into the clear blue sky.

She breathed in the smell of pine and fresh Colorado air.

"You're not in Florida anymore." That, she decided, was another blessing from her job loss.

Delighted to be outside, Baloo trotted next to her, head high. A few blocks later he stopped to sniff the base of a blue-and-white rectangle sign. Olivia didn't have to circle around to the other side to read the words scrolled across the silhouette of a church with a tall steeple. She knew them by heart. *Village Green, Colorado. Founded 1899. Population: 15,902. Elevation: 4,984.*

After ten years of school and work and clawing her way up the corporate ladder, she was back where she started. A little shattered, a bit heartbroken, but not beaten.

In no particular hurry now, Olivia let the dog take the lead. He sniffed a tree, paid avid attention to several bushes, all the while tugging her in the direction of a bubbling, three-tiered fountain at the center of Hawkins Park, named after the town's founder, Jonathan Hawkins.

Seemingly tuckered out by the time they arrived

at the marble monstrosity, Baloo settled at her feet, then shut his eyes and set in for a short nap.

Olivia was about to sit on the fountain's ledge when a puppy shot past her at lightning speed. The furry missile crested a small hill to her right, spun around, then sped back toward her.

Two young girls wearing matching white shorts and red T-shirts raced after him. "Samson, stop right now," one of them yelled while the other girl shouted, "Come back here."

Ears flat against his head, stubby legs pumping hard, Samson darted right, then left, then right again. In their haste to catch him, the girls tumbled over one another, landing in a heap. *"Sam-sooooooooon."*

Ignoring the call, the animal whizzed past the pile of tangled arms and legs, his bubblegum-pink tongue flapping in the wind.

Before Olivia could grab him, the puppy took a flying leap. He cleared the fountain's ledge and splashed down with a belly-busting splat.

He sank to the bottom like a stone.

Weren't dogs supposed to be able to swim?

With the girls' panicked shrieks in her ears, Olivia scooped the puppy out of the water. He came up wriggling and twisting, little legs running in the air.

"Calm down," she ordered.

Samson continued his antics, jetting water in every direction, including across the front of Olivia's shirt.

Laughing despite the impromptu bath, she held on tight and studied the animal through narrowed eyes. Seriously cute, she decided as she took in the plump belly, short tawny fur and adorable black face.

When he stopped thrashing she put him on the grass. Mindful of his earlier behavior, she kept her hands on his back, poised to snatch him up again if he attempted an escape.

He shook off the excess water, and immediately instigated a wrestling match with Baloo. The good-natured dog obliged the little troublemaker by rolling onto his back so Samson could climb up.

Olivia shifted her attention to the two young girls skidding to a stop beside her. By their height and size, she guessed their age to be somewhere around eight or nine years old. Nearly the same age as her ex-boyfriend's daughter, Kenzie. The thought brought such pain Olivia had to close her eyes until the moment passed.

"You saved Samson," one of the two sobbed.

Tears wavered in the other girl's eyes. "We were so worried we wouldn't catch him. He got away really fast."

Even without the identical clothing, Olivia pegged them for twins. They had the same long, pale blond hair, pretty features and arresting golden-brown eyes.

Something about those eyes sparked a memory, one that shimmered just out of reach.

Olivia glanced around. Where were their parents?

The girls were too young to be in the park alone. She plucked the puppy off Baloo and held him out. "Looking for this?"

"Oh, thank you." Blinking away her tears, the girl on Olivia's left took the dog, uncaring he was still wet. Now that the puppy was no longer harassing him, Baloo rolled back to his stomach and continued his nap.

"You look familiar." The girl holding the puppy angled her head. "Do we know you?"

"I don't think so. I've only just—"

"Megan, Molly," a deep, masculine voice rang out from the hilltop behind the girls. There was a note of concern in the rich baritone, one Olivia hoped she alleviated with a brief wave of her hand.

His steps quickened, eating up the ground in long, sure strides. A thousand thoughts collided together in her mind. She knew that purposeful walk, that handsome face, that wind-tousled hair the color of sandy, Florida beaches.

Connor Mitchell. Dressed in cargo shorts and a faded blue T-shirt.

What was her brother's partner in their family medical practice doing here, in the middle of a workday?

Olivia's gaze met Connor's across the lawn, and she immediately recognized the similarity with the two girls standing beside her, especially around the eyes. Even with his worried gaze, that was one good-looking man heading her way, as athletic and self-assured as she remembered.

Connor had been her brother's best friend since before she could remember. He'd always been confident, kind and so blissfully unaware of his masculine appeal. During high school, Olivia had found herself weaving secret teenage dreams, with him playing the starring role.

That had been a very long time ago.

Yet memories took hold of her. Stupid, girlish hopes and dreams for a boy far too old for her—a full five years—who hadn't noticed she was alive. He'd been too stuck on his childhood sweetheart, a woman he'd married right out of college. Shelly, Sheila, something like that. She'd died several years ago, leaving Connor a widower. And—as evidenced by the two girls standing beside her with those same striking Mitchell eyes—a single dad.

Relieved to find his daughters safe and the puppy no longer running loose, Connor let out an audible whoosh of air. The girls had darted away so fast he'd lost sight of them for a few terrifying minutes. Anything could have happened in that amount of time. The possibilities made him shudder.

Thankfully, nothing bad had occurred.

No doubt the woman standing beside the twins had played a large part in that. Gratitude nearly had him stumbling over his own feet.

He locked his gaze with hers and felt the blow

of shocked recognition like a punch to his gut. His feet ground to a halt far too close to her. He took a step back. "Olivia?"

"Hello, Connor." She gave him a slow, tentative smile that was a little shaky around the edges and yet devastatingly pretty. Ethan's baby sister was all grown up.

"Hello, Olivia." His voice sounded rusty and slightly stunned.

Who could blame him for his reaction? He had no way of knowing the shy, awkward teenager would become a woman of extraordinary beauty. How *could* he have known?

Olivia hadn't come home since taking a job in... Connor couldn't remember where. Somewhere in the South, he thought, but the specific location escaped him. It was possible Ethan had never told him. His medical partner was a man of few words.

Therein lay the problem. If Ethan had told Connor more about his sister, he would have been better prepared. Instead, he was stuck staring, struggling to reconcile his memory of the girl Olivia had been and the woman she'd become.

Little Olivia Scott had become a very attractive woman. The doll-like features had matured considerably. Her thick, mahogany hair hung in loose waves past her shoulders now.

A snarl of multilayered, complicated emotions surfaced, urging Connor to turn around and forget he ever ran into her today.

"Daddy?" Megan moved to him, tugged on his hand. "You know this lady?"

Connor shook himself free of Olivia's gaze and focused on his daughter. Sometimes it hurt to look at either of the twins. Both girls resembled Sheila. They had her same small build, delicate features and light blond hair.

Their eyes, however, were all his. Mitchell eyes, a trait that had been passed down through several generations. Or so his mother always said.

That wasn't the point.

What was the point?

"This is Olivia," he said at last, glancing back at her. "Miss Olivia Scott."

"Scott?" Molly's forehead creased in puzzlement. "Like Dr. Ethan?"

"That's right." Olivia answered his daughter before Connor could. "I'm Dr. Ethan's little sister."

Not so little anymore, he thought. Not only had the round, girlish features matured, but her voice had deepened since he'd last seen her. It was husky now, somehow softer, an appealing alto that made him think…

What?

Feeling slightly ambushed, Connor took another step back. Away from the sweet kid who was no longer his best friend's off-limits little sister, but a grown woman.

It felt wrong even noticing.

Out of the corner of his eye, he saw Megan bobble the squirming puppy. Welcoming the distraction, Connor reached out, catching the reckless mutt midair before tucking him under his arm like a football.

"Olivia. These are my daughters." He angled his head to the right, "Molly, and—" he hitched his chin to his left "—Megan."

"We're twins," Molly told her with no small amount of pride.

Olivia nodded. "I noticed."

She gave the girls a warm smile, but Connor noted she wasn't as calm as she appeared. Her breath was coming a little too quickly. She seemed nervous.

Because of him?

He cleared his throat.

"And this scoundrel—" he jiggled the puppy, earning him a happy yip "—is Samson, the newest member of the Mitchell household. He slipped out of his collar, which, as you can see, is still attached to this." Connor lifted the leash in his other hand. "Apparently, I failed to cinch the buckle tight enough."

"Ah." Olivia reached out and scratched the puppy behind his ears. "I've never seen an animal this short and…um…*round* move quite so fast."

"He's fat but has lots of hidden moves." Most of which Connor could live without.

The puppy had been his daughters' idea and an added responsibility to his already full life, especially now that he and Ethan had discussed expanding their practice to include Saturday hours and two evenings a week.

Even without the added workload, as much as the girls tried to take care of their new dog, and they did try, they simply had no experience with pets. The bulk of the responsibility fell on Connor.

Dropping her hand, Olivia studied the puppy with laughing eyes. "I can only imagine what this little guy is capable of when you turn your back."

Connor could give her a dissertation on the topic. "You have no idea."

They shared a smile solely between them. For a brief moment, Connor felt the tension drain from his shoulders and the ache in his heart loosen just a bit. The sensation left him oddly shaken, as had this entire meeting.

He cleared his throat again.

Although the shyer of his two daughters, Megan moved in close to Olivia and tugged on her arm. "You're very pretty."

"Well, thank you. So are you."

"What about me?" Molly asked, squirming in next to her sister.

Eyes crinkling at the edges, Olivia pretended to consider the question carefully. "You are easily as pretty as your sister."

Both girls laughed.

Connor did, too. For the first time in days—months—he wasn't worried about tight schedules, or running late, or forgetting something important. The girls were safe. The puppy found. And Olivia Scott was back in town.

Chapter Two

Standing close enough to make out the warm blend of bronze, amber and gold in Connor's eyes, Olivia quietly studied him. Sure, he was good-looking. *Really* good-looking. But that wasn't the reason for her sudden silence. It was the inexplicable desire to offer him comfort, as if she could somehow provide him with a place of rest from the outside world.

That made no sense.

The man was in the prime of his life. Strong, athletic, capable. Yet Olivia detected a hint of sorrow in him, a sorrow she understood all too well.

The slight sting she felt in her heart she attributed to missing her parents. Even now, over ten years after their car accident, the pain was still with her, would probably always be with her.

Did Connor suffer something similar?

How could he not? He'd lost his wife to cancer.

Olivia wished she could soothe away his grief,

as he'd once done for her that day after her parents' funeral.

Did he remember the momentary solace he'd given her with his kind words?

Out of the corner of her eye, Olivia could see his daughters watching her closely. She understood what they'd lost. But Olivia had enjoyed time with her mother for seventeen years. These girls had spent far less with theirs. The unfairness struck her. She smiled down at them.

They smiled back.

Shifting beside her, Connor drew Olivia's attention back to him. He wasn't looking at her, though. He was focused on his daughters. "Girls, it's time to go."

The arguments began immediately.

He shut them down with a look. "Say goodbye to Miss Olivia."

A little grumbling ensued before Megan stepped close to Olivia and looked up. "Bye, Miss Olivia."

Miss Olivia. Her heart tripped. Kenzie had called her that, too.

Olivia banished the thought, and focused only on the two girls staring up at her. They were at such a great age, when they still looked up to adults and chose obedience more often than not.

"It was nice to meet you, Megan." Olivia circled her gaze to include the girl's sister. "And you as well, Molly."

Molly's eyes rounded in response. "You can tell us apart?"

The surprise was understandable. On first glance the girls were identical. But on closer inspection, Molly held herself with more confidence. Her smile also came quicker, and with a mischievous glint in her eye. "Well, yes. I can."

"That's really..." Molly seemed to search for the right word "...*cool*."

"Yeah," Megan agreed. "Supercool."

Connor set the puppy on the ground and reattached the collar. His elegant, efficient movements reminded Olivia of an artist's expert strokes across a canvas. He had such nice hands, doctor's hands. Steady, confident, yet gentle.

Still not looking at her, he gave the puppy's collar a final check and then rose to his full height—all six feet two inches of casually clad male in those well-worn cargo shorts and a faded T-shirt. He was tall enough that Olivia had to tip her head back to look into his face. The shock of those intense amber eyes focused on her sent her heart stuttering.

What was wrong with her? Why this strange visceral reaction to the man? This was Connor Mitchell, for goodness' sake. Her brother's best friend since before Olivia was born. Ethan's friend, she reminded herself, not hers. She hadn't actually spoken to him for years before today.

"It was good to see you, Olivia." He paused a

moment, his expression easy. "I'm sure our paths will cross again while you're in town."

"I…" She tensed, started to tell him she was probably home for good, then thought, *Why would he need to know that?* "I certainly hope so."

Even to her own ears, the words came out a little wistful.

And mortifying.

Hadn't she learned her lesson when it came to single dads with demanding professions and adorable daughters in need of a woman's love?

Having been ignored long enough, Samson gave a ferocious growl before initiating a vicious tug-of-war with his leash.

"Troublemaker," Connor muttered, but obliged the puppy with a few hard snatches.

Samson hunched low, growled deeper in his throat, then whipped his head back and forth with fast, hard jerks.

A reluctant laugh escaped Connor.

Olivia gave in to her own amusement. The puppy was hard not to like. "That is one big, bad dog in the making."

"So he wants us all to think."

Samson suddenly let go of the leash, looked around and then pounced on Baloo.

Olivia reached down to pry the puppy loose.

Connor bent over, as well. Their hands connected atop Samson's back. They both froze. Less than a heartbeat later Connor moved his hand and picked up Samson.

He passed the puppy off to Molly.

Holding the animal close, the girl divided a look between her father and Olivia. A speculative glint whispered across her gaze, but disappeared so quickly Olivia thought she might have imagined the whole thing.

She said goodbye to the twins, patted Samson on the head and watched as the entire family turned to go. A final wave in her direction from the twins, and they disappeared back over the hill.

Now that puppy teeth were no longer chomping on his ear, Baloo hopped to his feet with the agility of a dog half his age. Olivia absently scratched her fingernails down his back, earning her a canine sigh.

She sighed, too.

The Mitchells were such a beautiful family, yet she couldn't help feeling a little sad for them. Cancer had left Connor to raise two young girls on his own. With three older brothers in the medical profession, Olivia knew the long hours he endured.

Not that it was any of her concern.

"Come on, Baloo. Let's go home."

On the walk back to the house, one thought kept running through Olivia's mind. She'd come home just in time, putting her on the right path to finding her true purpose in life. A purpose she hadn't considered when she'd been working fourteen-hour days.

The possibilities stretching before her were both exciting and terrifying.

It was nearly noon by the time Olivia guided Baloo into the mudroom at the back of their house. At this hour she wouldn't run into any of her brothers.

Ethan was at the office seeing patients. Ryder was at Village Green Hospital where he shared E.R. duties with two other doctors. And Brody was out of the country working for Doctors Without Borders.

With the house to herself, Olivia could continue working her way through the list of Village Green businesses. She needed to determine if the type of tearoom she had in mind would be redundant or just what the town needed. No thoughts of single dads and or sweet little girls would be allowed in her head. Work, work and more work.

She'd just hung up Baloo's leash when she heard a deep, masculine voice. "Olivia? That you?"

Her throat tightened. Of course Ethan would come home for lunch today, since he was the one brother she wanted to avoid most. Not that she didn't adore him; of course she did. But he had a way of asking questions that struck at the heart of a matter. Questions she didn't have answers for yet. Her emotions were too raw, and her plans too sketchy.

The fact that she hadn't heard his approach was a bit annoying, but not entirely her fault. Ethan still moved with that creepy stealth he'd learned as an Army Ranger.

She turned and smiled at him. Dressed in navy blue dress pants and a white button-down, he looked very much like the successful doctor he was. As with all her brothers, the stark contrast of his black hair and light blue eyes turned more than a few female heads, including most of Olivia's friends.

"Hey," she said, hoping she'd caught him on his way out. "I took Baloo for a walk. I'm assuming that was okay."

"Sure." He nodded, smiling. "He needs more exercise than I can give him."

Now that the pleasantries were over, she grabbed her laptop with the sole intention of heading somewhere else—anywhere else—to continue her fact-finding expedition. "Well, now that I brought him home, I'm heading out again."

"You just got back."

"I know, but—" she glanced over his shoulder, her gaze landing on the refrigerator "—we need groceries."

His eyebrows pulled together. "We have food in the house."

She rolled her eyes. Ethan was such a man. "Bottled water and cold pizza do not qualify as food."

He ignored this observation and placed a hand on her shoulder. "Olivia. Come into the den. We'll talk and—"

"I really should get going." She shrugged out from under his grip, trying not to think about all she'd lost. The job. The perfect ready-made family that had seemed within her reach.

So she'd been downsized. So she and Warner hadn't worked out. Maybe her breakup and job loss had come at an opportune time. Maybe even Divine Intervention, God working good out of the bad in her life.

"Stop worrying about me, Ethan. I'm simply between jobs."

He considered this, considered her. "So you've said already." He lowered his voice to that soothing doctor octave he donned so well. "I know that's not the truth."

She opened her mouth to argue.

"Not the *full* truth, in any case."

She thought about the tearoom of her dreams, the particulars still fuzzy, yet also thrilling, in her mind. "It's a long story with a few twists and turns but eventually leading to a happy ending."

She would make sure of it.

"Tell me more. I have time." He checked the chunky wristwatch he'd worn ever since his days in the military. "I don't have to be back at the office for another half hour."

His tone was so calm, so reasonable, as if she could explain in thirty minutes or less why she didn't want to take another job in banking. Why she wanted to try something that would require a leap of faith.

"How about I tell you everything tonight when you get home from work?"

"I'm not coming straight home. I have a meeting in Denver."

"Tomorrow, then." She patted him on the arm, relieved she would have more time. "I'll stop by the office and catch you between patients."

Giving him no chance to respond, she quickly exited the house, shutting the door on whatever response he'd been about to give.

Thanks to the tiny menace in a fur suit, Connor spent the rest of his day off in the emergency room, where he and the girls waited for news on Samson's latest victim—their housekeeper, Carlotta.

The puppy had escaped his crate and had proceeded to bolt through the house. With the twins giving chase, Samson had eventually darted into the kitchen and slid directly under Carlotta's foot, the one attached to her bad knee.

She'd gone down hard.

One look had told Connor he didn't have the necessary equipment to treat her injury at home, or at the office. Hence this unexpected trip to Village Green Hospital's E.R.

Connor would have joined Carlotta in the exam room, but she'd insisted he stay with the girls. He'd relented when Megan's eyes had filled with tears and Ryder Scott, the doctor on duty, had promised to give Connor an update as soon as he knew more.

While the twins watched television, Connor retrieved his phone from his back pocket and thumbed through his contact list. If Carlotta's injury was as bad as he suspected, he would need alternative child care.

"Daddy?"

He lifted his head.

Megan's bottom lip trembled. "You're not going to make us get rid of Samson, are you?"

"Not a chance, sweetheart." He pulled her into a one-arm hug. "He's part of the family now." For better or worse.

So far, it had been mostly worse.

Eyes full of worry, Molly drew alongside her sister. "Samson didn't mean to hurt Carlotta."

Connor gave her a reassuring smile. "No, sweetheart, he didn't."

He wanted to say more, explain that the puppy needed obedience school stat, but Ryder joined them in the waiting room. The other doctor's tight expression confirmed Connor's suspicions. The news was bad.

He stood. Megan rushed past him and tugged on Ryder's sleeve. "Is Carlotta going to be okay?"

Ryder glanced at Connor before answering, "Sure is."

The other doctor smiled down at Megan. The gesture wiped away the tension on his face and relaxed his features, reminding Connor of the man's younger sister. All the Scotts looked alike, but this one favored Olivia the most, right down to the blue-blue eyes, the color of the Colorado sky.

Connor had been thinking a lot about Olivia since their unexpected reunion this morning. Hard not to, since his daughters had chattered nonstop about her all the way home from the park.

She'd certainly made an impression on them.

The image of Olivia's eyes crinkling around the edges when she smiled at them still hovered in the back of his mind.

"Hey, kiddo." Ryder tugged on Megan's ponytail, the only hairstyle Connor had mastered in his four years of solo parenting. "No need for tears. Your housekeeper's going to live. She just busted up her knee."

Connor tried not to groan at the description. "How badly *busted up* are we talking?"

"Broken kneecap, torn ACL. The orthopedic surgeon is with her now. He's suggesting immediate surgery."

Translation: months of recovery time.

The girls' summer break had barely begun. Connor stuffed his phone back in his pocket. "I'd like to see her now."

Ryder hooked a thumb over his left shoulder. "Third room on the left."

"Be right back." He stayed only long enough to determine how Carlotta was feeling, promise he'd take care of any medical bills not covered by insurance and assure her she had a job when her knee healed.

As soon as he and the girls arrived home from the hospital, Connor went to work on his child-care dilemma. He made the first call to his sister Avery a recent college grad home for a few months before she started medical school in the fall.

She answered on the second ring. "Hey, bro. What's up?"

After he explained the situation, she clicked her tongue in sympathy. "Ouch, poor Carlotta. Tell me what I can do to help."

"Can you watch the girls tomorrow?"

"I can watch them all summer if necessary."

"It won't come to that." He glanced out into the backyard. The twins were attempting to run off the puppy's seemingly never-ending energy. *Good luck with that.*

"I mean it, Connor."

"I know, Avery, and I appreciate it." He tightened his hold on the phone. "But I promised you experience in the office before you start medical school, and I'm going to keep my word."

Resolved to find a solution that would work for everyone, he ended the call.

Closing his eyes, he wiped the back of his hand across his mouth. He was suddenly bone-tired, as if the long, endless days he'd endured since Sheila's death were finally catching up with him.

He missed his wife, missed her company and the deep, abiding friendship they'd shared since the third grade. Four years since her death, he was past the worst of his grief and moving on with his life. Some days were easier than others; most were just hard work.

He would tackle this latest problem as he did all the others. One detail at a time. He spent the rest of the night either on the phone or waiting for someone to return his call.

Unfortunately, he arrived at his office the next day with his child-care problem still unresolved. Connor would not rely solely on his sister. He would figure out another solution.

His mind on several options, he headed toward the east wing of the building where he had his personal office space. He stepped across the threshold and...

Stopped cold.

Olivia Scott stood beside his desk, seemingly absorbed with the task of writing on a piece of paper beneath her hand.

Connor's heart took a quick, hard thump. Ethan's sister looked like summer in a pair of white jeans, a fancy blue top and high-heeled sandals.

His mind went momentarily blank. "Olivia?"

She looked up and smiled. "Oh, Connor. Hi. I was just leaving you a note. Guess I don't have to now." She lifted the piece of paper beneath her fingertips, then tossed it in the trash.

She shifted a step closer. Her scent, a pleasant mix of lavender and vanilla, was very female and more than a little distracting. "Aren't you going to ask me why I'm here?"

"Okay…" He angled his head, swallowed. "Why are you here?" He swallowed again. "And why were you leaving me a note?"

Leaning back against his desk, she rested her hands on either side of her. "I have a proposition for you."

He simply stared at her, uncertain how to respond to that.

"I heard your housekeeper injured her knee yesterday." Her gaze turned somber. "Ryder told me about the accident when he came home last night."

Ah.

"I figure this probably puts you in a bind when it comes to child care for your daughters this summer."

"It does." He rubbed the back of his neck. "My sister is helping out for now. But I need to find a more permanent solution, at least until Carlotta's knee heals."

Olivia's pretty smile returned. "That's where I come in."

He waited for the rest.

Her smile brightened even more. "I know the perfect person to watch your girls this summer."

He tried to focus on her words, not on the fact that his heartbeat had picked up speed, or that he experienced a flash of insight, as if he were on the verge of something life-changing. "Who did you have in mind?"

"Me."

Chapter Three

For the second time since entering his office, Connor found himself rendered speechless. Had Olivia just offered to watch his daughters for the entire summer?

He swept his gaze over her face, measuring, gauging. The teasing light had fled from her eyes, replaced by a look of unmistakable sincerity. There was also a twinge of excitement he didn't understand.

There had to be something he was missing.

"Don't you already have a job? In…" He tried to remember what she'd studied in college. Surely Ethan had told him. Marketing? Finance? "Banking?"

She glanced away a moment and sighed. "That's right. For a number of years I helped failing companies with debt consolidation and financial restructuring."

"Impressive."

She shrugged. "Mostly just a lot of number crunching."

"I'm sure there's more to it than that." He ran a thriving medical practice. He had a good idea what it took to keep afloat in a tight economy.

"Anyway, I'm not doing that anymore. I'm looking into other options for the future. In the meantime, I'm free to help you out."

"Are you saying you're unemployed?"

"I'm saying I'm in Village Green while I consider my next career move." She didn't expand. Nor, Connor noted, had she addressed his question directly.

Could this meeting get any more confusing?

Her smile flashed again, quick and devastating. That smile, it made him think of silver linings at the end of a long, dark day.

"This is a God thing, you know, my being available to watch your daughters like this."

Connor had no comment. He'd given up on God years ago. Or, more accurately, God had given up on him. It hadn't mattered that he'd prayed nonstop for his wife's return to health. Not only had she not gotten better; Sheila had died slowly, painfully. Even his efforts to provide her comfort at the end had failed.

He did his best raising the twins on his own. But Molly and Megan needed a woman in their lives, one who would love them as much as Sheila did. That's why he'd started dating, though he wasn't really in the game, merely attempting to take the first step. A lunch every now and then when he had time, which was hardly ever.

Olivia moved closer, the sound of her heels on the wood floor breaking through his thoughts. "I'll take excellent care of your girls."

This seemed too good to be true.

He opened his mouth to respond, but Olivia smiled at him again, a big toothy grin that gave him pause. Having her in his home every day might not be wise.

He shoved his fingers through his hair and carefully stripped his voice of emotion. "Let's say I agree to your offer. When would you be available to start work?"

Her earnest gaze met his. "Immediately."

"What's the rush?"

"No rush."

He stared at her.

She never blinked, not once. But he got the sense she wasn't being completely candid with him.

"What's in it for you?"

Now she blinked. Twice. Her hesitation was obvious. But then she looked at him again, smiled and said, "Let me take care of your daughters for you, Connor."

She grabbed his hand and a new kind of alertness took hold of him. "I promise to do right by them," she whispered, releasing his hand. "And you."

He didn't doubt her sincerity. But what did a bank exec know about kids?

As if reading his mind, Olivia continued.

"Back in high school I earned enough money babysitting to buy my first car. I love kids. Always have, especially girls around your daughters' age. I—" She cut herself off and blinked slowly, as if the words were painful to say. "I really do love kids."

Her voice held a strange mix of sincerity and reserve, with a hint of hope underneath. Connor knew the feeling. He felt poised on the brink of something new himself, something life-altering.

Some of the knots in his gut unraveled. Then he remembered that watching his daughters was only part of the job description. "You'll have to take on Samson, too."

This seemed to amuse her. "How bad can one tiny puppy be?"

"Bad enough to put my housekeeper in the hospital."

Olivia's expression sobered. "Right."

Reaching out to him, she laid her hand on his arm. Something inside him shifted under her gentle touch.

"Don't worry, Connor." She chuckled. "I know my way around dogs just as well as I do little girls."

The selfish part of him wanted to hire her on the spot. The wiser part of him whispered a warning to hold off making a final decision. She might have babysat in high school, but that was a decade ago.

Even if she'd been a professional nanny all her adult life, something about Olivia Scott dug past the efficient facade he relied on to get him through the day. If he hired her, Connor could very well lose the fragile balance he'd carefully put in place.

But he couldn't deny the fact that his daughters liked Olivia. They'd made that perfectly clear after their time with her in the park yesterday. All things considered, her offer might be the perfect solution to his child-care problems.

Still, Connor hesitated.

"What if we do this on a trial basis?" she asked.

"How would that work?"

"I'll watch the girls for a few days. At the end of that time we'll reevaluate the situation." She placed her hands on her hips. "If any of us aren't happy with the arrangement, and that includes your daughters, then I'll walk away."

He couldn't say why the idea of her walking away bothered him, so he did a mental dance around the thought and focused on the matter at hand. "That could work."

"If our arrangement doesn't suit either of us, then I'll help you find my replacement."

"Before I agree to this trial run..." Was he really considering this? "I have a stipulation."

"Only one?"

His lips twitched at her response. When was the last time he'd laughed? Really laughed? Yesterday, he realized, in Hawkins Park when Olivia Scott had saved an out-of-control puppy from possible drowning and made his daughters smile.

"You mentioned a stipulation?" she asked.

"Ethan has to agree."

"What? Why?" Her eyes narrowed. "My brother has no say in what I can or cannot do."

Maybe not. But as the oldest in a family of five siblings, *and* the only male, Connor knew firsthand the mind-set of a protective older brother. If their roles were reversed, and the other doctor was having this conversation with one of Connor's sisters, he'd have a few reservations.

"Ethan is my business partner and friend. He needs to be okay with this. Talk to him. If he has no objections, then we'll give it a try."

She expelled an audible breath. "All right. I'll speak to him, but only because you asked. I would never want to cause problems for you at work."

With a determined gleam in her eye, she moved past him. "This won't take long."

Knowing how protective Ethan was of his one and only sister, Connor doubted that.

A rush of impatience surged through Olivia. What should have been a brief conversation was taking twice as long as it should. Waiting for her unusually long-winded brother to wind down, she slid a covert glance around his office. Nice. Masculine, tasteful, well organized.

Very efficient. Very Ethan.

Her gaze landed on a picture of him in full military gear, his arm slung over a woman's shoulders. Even dressed in battle fatigues, she was a pretty girl, her smile nearly model-perfect. The two looked happy. They looked *together*.

Where was the other soldier now? And why had Ethan never mentioned her?

Observant to a fault, he caught her looking at the photo. With a swipe of his hand, he turned the picture facedown on the desk. The lines around his eyes seemed to cut deeper when he looked back at Olivia.

"You're a banker, Liv, not a nanny."

Oh, joy, they were back to that. "I babysat almost every night back in high school," she reminded him a third—or was it a fourth?—time. She could tell him about all the time she'd spent with Kenzie when it had been Warner's weekend with his daughter. How she'd loved and taken care of the girl as if she were her own.

"That was years ago, Liv. And besides—" He crossed his arms over his chest "—I thought you were only home for a short visit until the job at the bank in Denver opens up again."

That had been true when she'd set out from Florida. She'd had every intention of taking a banking position similar to the one she'd left. But Olivia had experienced a change of heart on the cross-country drive. How did she tell Ethan she believed the Lord had given her a new passion to replace the old? One that would require considerable planning and a very large leap of faith?

Remembering her father's long-ago advice, Olivia shifted to offense now that her defense was running weak. "It's my Christian duty to help out a friend in need."

"Connor isn't your friend. He's mine."

"Same difference." She snapped her shoulders back. "If we're finished here I should get back—"

He pointed a finger at her. "You're hiding something."

"You're paranoid."

"Now you're deflecting the conversation back on me." He stuffed his hands in his pockets. "What's going on, Olivia?"

Why did he have to care so much, see so much, when all she wanted to do was focus on the future, not the devastating events of the past that had brought her home in the first place?

As much as she wanted to run from this conversation, to pretend she wasn't still raw from all the losses she'd suffered, she knew she couldn't keep putting her brother off.

"I'm not sure I want to continue in my chosen profession." There. She'd said it. The truth was out at last. "In fact, I want to take some time to think through my options. *All* my options."

"Are you telling me you quit your job in Jacksonville before you—"

"I was downsized," she admitted.

"Olivia." Tenderness filled his gaze, a look that spoke of genuine affection and brotherly concern. "Why didn't you tell Ryder and me when you first came home? Why didn't you just—"

"Admit that I've been chasing the wrong dreams," *and the wrong man,* "for all the wrong reasons? That I'm about to turn thirty with nothing to show for my life?"

No job. No family.

Nothing.

"Olivia, you're the most capable woman I know." Hands on her shoulders, he squeezed gently. "And the smartest of all us Scotts put together. It's only a matter of time before you're back in the workforce, killing it with all the other financial whizzes in whatever direction you choose to take."

Needing a moment to process her brother's unfailing support, she glanced out his office window. The view was spectacular on this side of the building, full of snowcapped mountain peaks, yellow-leafed aspens and thick Colorado pines. "I appreciate your confidence. But until I figure out what's next for me, I'm free to watch Connor's daughters. That's what we financial whizzes call a win-win."

He didn't crack a smile at her joke. If anything, the worry in his gaze deepened. "Be sure this is what you want to do before you commit to watching the girls. It'll be too hard for Connor to find another replacement if you change your mind."

She wasn't going to change her mind. Even if

taking the position might be painful at first, a reminder of all she'd lost when she broke it off with Warner, two little girls needed her. "That's excellent advice. Now, if we're through, I need to find Connor and give him the good news."

"Olivia—"

She shut the door on the rest of his words. *Not running away,* she told herself. She was merely walking away very quickly. At least she'd told Ethan the truth about her job loss and her desire to consider a different career path altogether.

Feeling marginally better, she wound her way back through the twisting corridors of the building.

Head down, her mind on all the things she and the girls would do together over the summer, she failed to pay attention to her surroundings. Which probably explained why she ran into an immovable wall of muscles wrapped inside a white lab coat.

She mumbled a quick apology, then promptly lost her balance.

Connor steadied her. "Easy, now."

She clutched at his arms. "Sorry."

"You already said that." His voice sounded strained, much as hers had a moment before.

"Oh…right. Anyway." Cheeks on fire, she took that much-needed step back and looked everywhere but at the man towering over her.

Maybe Ethan was right. Maybe she should take another day to consider the ramifications of working for Connor.

You won't be working for him, she reminded herself. Not in the strictest sense of the word. She'd be taking care of his daughters while he was at the office. In her free time she would work on her business plan and test out new recipes, maybe even try a few on Connor's family. As far as she was concerned, that was the real win-win.

"How did your talk with your brother go?"

"Really great." She let out a soft sigh. "He couldn't be more on board if it had been his idea."

"It went that badly, huh?"

She bristled. "I didn't say it went badly."

"You didn't have to. I'll be right back." He set out in the direction of Ethan's office.

She stopped him with a touch to his arm. "Please don't."

"He's my partner, Olivia. I won't put a rift in our relationship simply to solve my current child-care problem." He closed his hand over hers. "Nor will I jeopardize your relationship with him, either."

How sweet. And really thoughtful. But completely unnecessary. "Ethan's not opposed to me helping you out." She tugged her hand free from beneath his. "He merely suggested I take a day to think it over."

"That's not a bad idea."

He was taking Ethan's side in this? "I appreciate your predicament, Connor, I really do, but my brother will come around eventually. He's already halfway there."

"I still want to discuss this with him."

"I don't see why it matters."

"Because Connor understands the value of loyalty and friendship," Ethan said, maneuvering around her to stand shoulder-to-shoulder with his longtime friend and partner.

Her brother's creepy stealth was going to get him decked one day. Probably by her.

And there they stood. Two superior male specimens. Nearly the same height and build, Ethan's dark to Connor's light, the solidarity in their longstanding friendship evident in their similar stances.

She frowned at them both.

"Whatever this bro code is between you two—" she flicked her wrist from one to the other "—it doesn't change the fact that Connor needs a temporary nanny for his daughters. And I'm available."

Both men looked at her, then at each other. Something passed between them before Ethan lifted a shoulder. "It's up to you, Con."

Olivia breathed a sigh of relief, ready to celebrate the win-win, until she realized *Con* hadn't given his answer.

"Well?" she asked him.

Another glance at her brother, then… "Let's try it."

Yes. "Well, then. If you have no objection, I could go over to your house this morning." When he started to speak, she added, "It'll be easier for the girls if I learn their routine while your sister is still around."

He went silent again, his eyebrows drawing together.

Reminding herself she wasn't in charge, yet, she took a deep breath and forced her words out more carefully than before. "I didn't mean to overstep. I merely assumed you would want me to start as soon as possible."

"I don't have a problem with you heading over to my house this morning." He slipped his hands into his pockets and rocked back on his heels. "Actually, it's not a bad idea. I'll call Avery and let her know to expect you."

"Excellent." Olivia hadn't seen Avery in years. It'd be nice to catch up. "I'll call you when I'm through and we can iron out the details of my job duties."

"Good enough."

She turned to go.

"Olivia?"

She looked over her shoulder, and nearly tripped. The impact of Connor's golden eyes sliding over her face was like a physical blow. It didn't help matters that Ethan had gone unnaturally silent, watching them interact with those all-seeing Ranger eyes. "Yes?"

Connor angled his head. "Do you know where I live?"

"Uh...no."

Lips twitching, he rattled off his address. Why did that sound so familiar?

This time, when she turned to leave, neither man

tried to stop her. They did, however, follow her into the parking lot, neither speaking, both watching her closely.

Refusing to be intimidated, she climbed into her car. Ethan's earlier warning knocked around in her brain. *Be sure this is what you want to do.*

Oh, she was sure. Very sure.

Chapter Four

Standing beside Ethan in the parking lot, Connor watched Olivia zip away in a sporty red BMW. The car was a perfect fit for the woman she'd become—sophisticated, chic, with an unexpected kick under the hood. The cheery wave she tossed through the open sunroof made him smile.

Thinking of her with his girls felt good. It felt right.

For an alarming moment, he teetered between past and present, wondering if he'd made a mistake hiring Olivia.

Ethan clapped him on the back. "Your daughters will love my sister. She's a natural with kids."

Connor remembered the way she'd interacted with the girls in the park yesterday, how easy she'd been with them and how quickly she'd been able to tell them apart.

Olivia seemed the perfect solution to his child-care problems, and a good fit with his daughters.

Still, Connor couldn't rid himself of the notion that he'd just made his life more complicated rather than less. "Hard to think of your sister as a high-powered banker rescuing companies from financial ruin."

"Surprised all three of us when she chose a business career instead of pursuing medicine." Ethan slipped his hands into his pockets, stared out over the parking lot as if lost in thought. "The Scotts have been doctors for three generations."

The Mitchells had been in the profession nearly as long, with one glaring exception. The first doctor in Connor's family had been a woman. The rest of his cousins were ranchers, an even longer family tradition than medicine.

"With Olivia's love of kids, I thought she'd go into pediatrics."

"And with your trauma experience I thought you'd join Ryder in the E.R. when you left the military."

Although his shrug was casual, Ethan's face went blank, like a switch turning off.

Connor didn't press. He never did. But he couldn't help wondering what had happened to his friend on that last tour of duty in Afghanistan.

"Doesn't matter why," he said aloud. "You're stuck with me now, treating nothing more complicated than runny noses, an occasional spider bite and a broken bone or two. Riveting stuff."

Ethan laughed, as Connor knew he would. They saw worse, sometimes much worse, but nothing compared to what his friend had encountered in a war zone.

"Speaking of broken bones." Ethan shook his head. "Robbie Anderson is in Exam Room 2."

Again? "Which one this time?"

"Left tibial shaft. The kid was lucky, though. It's a stable fracture and the fibula wasn't damaged at all."

"I suppose that's something."

As they reentered the building, Ethan added, "There's considerable swelling, so I'll have to splint the leg first, see about a cast later. Tasha's prepping him now."

Good. A former search and rescue coordinator, the nurse knew her way around broken bones.

"You take 1." Ethan jerked his chin at the closed door farther down the hallway. "The patient specifically requested you."

Not quite sure what he saw in the other man's eyes, Connor reached for the chart in the door holder.

Chuckling softly, Ethan disappeared into Exam Room 2.

Alone in the hallway, Connor gave the chart in his hand a cursory glance. He groaned softly. The patient behind door Number 1 was Lacy Hargrove, Village Green's self-proclaimed most eligible bachelorette. No denying the young divorcée was beautiful, in an over-the-top, plastic sort of way. She was also on the prowl for husband number three.

Connor groaned again.

The woman made him uneasy. She made most

men in town uneasy, even the stalwart, battle-toughened, Ethan Scott. No wonder the coward had pawned her off on Connor.

Hitting his cue perfectly, Ethan stuck his head out of Exam Room 2. "Tag, buddy, you're it."

Connor snarled. "Anyone ever mention you have a mean streak?"

"Only every other person who meets me."

Following the GPS voice commands on her phone, Olivia swung her car onto Aspen Way. Anticipation building, she inched along, verifying addresses as she went. Each block she covered brought her closer to the edge of town. At the last house on the street, she slammed on the brakes.

Her mouth dropped open and waves of delight washed over her. Connor had bought Charity House.

The sprawling old home had once been an orphanage in the 1800s. Or rather, a baby farm, which was really just a fancy name for a place where prostitutes in the Old West sent their illegitimate children for a solid Christian upbringing.

Both the Scotts and the Mitchells had ancestors directly connected to the place. Some of the stories were legendary, others so far-fetched Olivia hadn't believed them for a moment.

Members of both families had worked at the orphanage, while others had married someone closely connected. All had lived out their faith, showing

God's grace to abandoned children and their prostitute mothers.

Smiling, Olivia swung her car onto the gravel road leading to the grand old mansion.

A sense of rightness filled her. This temporary nanny position came at a perfect time in her life. During the day, she would concentrate on taking care of Connor's daughters. Maybe even teach them how to cook while testing out new recipes. At night, she would work on her business plan, perfecting it until she was ready to present her idea to a bank or potential investor.

Win-win.

As long as she kept her heart firmly guarded and remembered her place in Connor's home.

The three-story house was undergoing renovations, as evidenced by the scaffolding. Even in its unfinished state, the home was something straight out of a fairy tale—whimsical in design, the sharp angles of the roof were softened by clinging wisteria, rounded windows and wrought-iron balconies.

Head full of damsels in distress and happily-ever-afters, Olivia parked her car at the end of the drive and climbed out. She'd barely commandeered the steps leading onto a lovely wraparound porch when the front door flew open. Out spilled a wild-eyed, frazzled young woman Olivia immediately recognized.

"Good morning, Avery."

"What's good about it?"

The poor girl looked so overwhelmed, so flustered that Olivia found herself wanting to lighten the mood as quickly as possible. "That's some kind of greeting after all these years."

Avery's face fell. "Oh, Olivia. I'm so sorry. I didn't mean that the way it sounded." Cheeks bright pink, her golden eyes round with remorse, she clasped Olivia's hands. "It's been a bit hectic this morning."

Aside from her flushed face, several blond locks had slipped out of her ponytail and now fluttered over her eyes.

"Are the girls giving you trouble?"

"Not even a little. They're wonderful. But that dog of theirs?" Avery executed an impressive eye-roll. "He's a walking nuisance on four pudgy legs."

Samson's latest victim. Unlike Carlotta's experience with the puppy, at least Avery only suffered a large case of frustration.

"Let's try this again." Avery blew a strand of hair off her face. Her smile came quicker now, fuller. "It's really great to see you. You look amazing."

"I was thinking the same about you." She squeezed her old friend's hand. "And the good news is—"

A loud crash from inside the house cut off the rest of her words.

"Samson, no." A panicked squeal followed the command. Then came the cringe-worthy statement "Not on the floor."

"Here we go again." Avery took off in a dead run.

Trailing after her, Olivia only had time for impressions as she rushed toward the back of the house. She noticed the décor and concluded that, much like the exterior, the interior was still a work in progress.

She caught up with Avery in the kitchen. She was on her hands and knees attacking Samson's latest magnum opus with quiet fervor and a handful of paper towels.

The culprit was nowhere in sight. Nor, Olivia noted, were the twins.

"Megan and Molly hustled the puppy outside, probably to keep me from killing him. I wouldn't have, you know." Avery tossed the soiled towels in the trash, then went to wash her hands in the sink. "I'd never hurt the little guy."

"Of course not." Olivia patted her hand in commiseration.

"He's just so full of…" Avery moved her shoulders as if trying to dislodge a heavy weight. "Energy."

That was one way of putting it.

"Well, I have good news. I have nothing pressing on my calendar today. I can stick around and observe or help or whatever for as long as you need me."

Avery leaned in close, nearly pressing her nose to Olivia's. "How long are you suggesting?"

"All day, if necessary."

"Woot!" Pumping her palms in the air, Avery wiggled her hips, twirled in a circle.

The rest of the day went by in a blur. To use

Avery's words, the girls were wonderful. And, yes, Samson was a nuisance. At least he was a cute nuisance, and easy enough to manage, once Olivia taught the stubborn little guy who was in charge. That had only taken three exhausting hours.

By midafternoon, Avery started making noise about needing to reread her anatomy and physiology notes before starting work in Connor's office. After checking with Connor, Olivia told Avery to go on home.

She was out the door in a flash.

Now, a few minutes shy of six, the girls were busy setting the table in the kitchen's breakfast nook while Olivia checked on the casserole she'd popped in the oven earlier. Satisfied it was cooking nicely, she carefully shut the oven door and looked around.

This must have been one of the first rooms Connor had renovated. Aside from the usual appliances, all top-of-the-line, there was an enormous refrigerator and a massive center island with a built-in grill.

She could do a lot of creating in a kitchen like this.

Sighing over the possibilities, she dragged her fingertip along the granite countertop, scooting around a slumbering Samson as she went. The puppy slept as hard as he played.

Smiling at him, she reached down to rub his upturned belly. The sound of a key turning in a lock had him leaping to his feet and bolting out of the kitchen.

"Daddy's home," Molly declared, chasing after the dog.

Megan joined the welcome-home party a half step later.

Olivia remained in the kitchen. She smoothed a hand over her hair, straightened the hem of her shirt, then checked her white jeans for stains and unwanted wrinkles.

Jeans don't wrinkle, she reminded herself. Feeling oddly out of sorts, she didn't know what to do with her hands.

What was wrong with her? She was usually so in control. Stubborn CEOs determined to drive their companies into financial ruin often required firm handling.

From the foyer, Connor's rumbling laugh mixed with his daughters' higher-pitched giggles. Olivia couldn't help smiling and her nerves instantly disappeared. It was just Connor out there in the hallway, laughing with his daughters.

By the time he joined her in the kitchen, her heartbeat had almost leveled out. Then he aimed those startling amber eyes in her direction and she nearly forgot to breathe.

"You didn't have to cut Avery loose."

"Actually—" she shot a meaningful look at Samson trotting in the room behind him "—I did."

Following the direction of her gaze, Connor winced. "Do I want to know?"

"Probably not."

Frowning, he picked up the puppy and tucked him under his arm. Olivia couldn't fault the move, definitely a safer place for the animal than on the floor.

"Smells good in here."

"It's chicken divan casserole. My own secret recipe."

The frown lines cut deeper across his forehead. "Cooking wasn't part of our deal."

Something in his tone put her on guard. "We don't actually have a deal yet, remember? And I like cooking, so no problem."

"I'd planned to order takeout tonight." His tone never varied, his eyes never left her face, but the stiff way he held his shoulders told its own story. He didn't like that she'd cooked for him and his family.

She had no idea why, but didn't think it was her place to ask. "I can put the casserole in the freezer. That way you and the girls can enjoy it another time."

An odd tension collected in the air between them, broken only when the twins entered the kitchen.

"Daddy, Daddy." Molly tugged on her father's arm. "Did Olivia tell you we helped make dinner?"

The smile Connor dropped on his daughter was full of affection, and much less forced than the one he'd given Olivia. "Sounds like fun."

"It was superfun." Megan pushed past her sister and came to stand next to Olivia. "We learned how to grate cheese and mix up biscuit dough from scratch and set the table properly."

"That's..." Connor shifted the puppy in his arms. "Nice."

The poor man looked shell-shocked. Again, she wondered why. "Connor?" Olivia angled her head at him. "Are you okay?"

"Sure, great." He seemed to visibly get hold of himself. Finally, he flashed a genuine smile at her. "And, no, you don't have to freeze the casserole. We'll eat it tonight."

He sounded sincere.

Yet something had upset him. A dozen possibilities came to mind, none of them good, all of them caused by her, which made little sense. He'd hired her to take care of his daughters; surely that included making meals. Why the concern?

Perhaps if she explained that she'd only been trying to make the evening easier for him by cooking dinner, he'd feel less agitated. Of course, that wasn't a conversation to be conducted in front of the girls.

"Dinner will be ready in a few minutes." She smiled down at Molly. "Why don't you and Megan take Samson out in the yard before we eat?"

"I guess we can do that." She took the puppy from her father, glanced over at her sister. "Come on, Megan, let's get this over with."

The other girl stayed firmly rooted to Olivia's side.

"Go on, sweetie." Olivia gave her a gentle push toward the back door. "You can put ice in the glasses when you get back."

"Okay." She dragged her feet all the way across the floor.

Olivia waited until the door shut behind the twins before addressing Connor again. "Did I cross a line?"

"No."

That was succinct. Straight to the point. And told her absolutely nothing. She pressed for more. "Would you rather I not teach the girls how to cook?"

"On the contrary." He let out a breath that sounded as weary as he looked. "I think it's a good idea. It's just..."

His words trailed off and he rubbed a hand over his face, but not before Olivia saw the inner conflict he couldn't quite hide. "What's wrong, Connor?"

He stared straight ahead, his expression closed. He appeared deep in thought, visibly debating something within himself. "You and I haven't discussed your specific job duties."

No, they hadn't. But that wasn't what had him looking as if she'd punched him in the chest. "I assumed my filling in for Carlotta would include meals, light housekeeping and—"

"You don't have to clean my house."

She jumped at his abrupt tone.

"I'll hire a service for that," he added more softly, almost apologetically.

"Connor, what is this really about?"

He flicked a glance toward the back door. The

gesture gave him a hunted look, as if he didn't want to be alone with her.

"I have a few more things to do before dinner's ready." She kept her voice light. Easygoing. Nothing to worry about here. Still, she couldn't escape a vague sense of rejection. "Why don't you go hang out with your daughters while I get everything ready in here?"

His chin jerked, very faintly, but she caught the gesture. And the hesitation. He had something more to say.

Whatever it was, Olivia didn't want to hear it right now.

"It's a beautiful evening." She subtly motioned toward the door, making sure to do so calmly, with very little fanfare. "It'd be a shame not to take advantage of the fresh air."

He nodded. Slowly. Then deliberately stepped around her, careful not to touch her as he passed by. Mildly hurt, she barely restrained herself from informing him she was up to date on all her cootie shots.

At the door, he stopped abruptly, turned around and moved back to her side. "Olivia?"

"Yes?"

He clasped both her hands in his. "I appreciate you making dinner tonight. You went above the call of duty. I…" He smiled into her eyes. "Thank you."

For a moment, Olivia thought her knees might give out. Desperate for some perspective, she lowered her head. And immediately connected her gaze with their joined hands.

Why did hers look so right wrapped inside his?

And why—*why*—did she have to notice something so small and inconsequential?

"Oh, Connor." She lifted her head to stare into his eyes. "You're so very welcome."

Chapter Five

While the twins played with their puppy in the backyard, Connor sat alone on the stoop and breathed in the clean, pine-scented air. The lawn needed cutting and the hedges could use a good trim. He'd get to both eventually. But not tonight.

Maybe over the weekend.

"Never enough time," he muttered, pressing his fingers to his temples. The gesture did nothing to relieve the pounding behind his eyes.

On a tight breath, he dropped his hands and focused on his daughters. Their unrestrained laughter soothed the ache in his heart, and slowed down his raging pulse. Unfortunately, his rambling thoughts didn't fall into line as easily.

Arriving home at night in time for dinner was one of the things he'd promised Sheila on her deathbed. The juggling necessary to follow through on that promise wasn't always easy, but always worth the effort.

Family first, family always, that had been Sheila's motto.

Connor's, too.

Or, at least, it was now. He had no regrets. His life was richer, fuller, for keeping his priorities straight.

But seeing how well Olivia fit in his home, how comfortable she'd looked in his kitchen, had been like a punch in the gut. And a stab to his heart. He couldn't explain why.

The dull drumming behind his eyes took on a mean edge.

Connor wanted his daughters to have a woman's influence in their lives, a mother figure even. But Olivia Scott?

He'd never thought of her that way.

Well, except that one time he'd forced himself to forget, because there had been nothing to remember.

Or so he'd told himself.

But, now, looking back, he wondered...

He'd been in his senior year at University of Colorado, home for a short visit before final exams. Sheila had just given him an ultimatum: Propose or let her go.

She'd been the love of his life, the only girl he'd ever dated. He'd never intended anything other than marrying her. But his plan had been to finish medical school before settling down.

Sheila hadn't wanted to wait.

Confused and angry at being pushed into a decision before he was ready, Connor had stopped by the Scott home to speak with Ethan. He'd needed his friend's perspective.

Ethan hadn't been home.

Olivia had. She'd been sixteen at the time, maybe seventeen, still a girl. But there'd been a moment when Connor had seen the promise of the woman she would become. It hadn't been attraction, not exactly, but it hadn't been indifference, either.

More like a...*hmmm*.

He'd felt the same shocked wonder again just now in the kitchen.

How did he reconcile the shift from mild curiosity to—

Samson scrambled into his lap, sufficiently averting his attention. The animal's paws were covered in wet, sticky mud, as now were Connor's khakis. He picked up the squirming bundle of tawny fur. The puppy's legs pumped hard.

Connor tightened his grip.

"Sorry, Daddy." Megan frowned at the dog. "He sort of fell in a mud puddle."

Connor gave a soft, humorless sigh. Samson sort of fell into a lot of mishaps. The dog was a walking, yipping disaster magnet.

Straining against Connor's hold, the mutt leaned forward and licked Connor's face. "Not cool."

Samson gave him another lick, followed by a big puppy grin.

"Really not cool."

Olivia slipped her head out the back door, saving the dog from a good scolding. "Dinner's ready."

"Be right there." Connor set the puppy on the ground, held him steady with a hand on his back. "Can one of you toss me a towel from the mudroom?"

"On it," Molly announced, shuffling past him.

"I'll get Samson's dinner ready," Megan offered.

"That'd be great."

The door slammed behind the girls. Then swung back open a second later. "Here you go, Daddy."

A rag sailed through the air. Connor caught it with one hand and immediately went to work wiping the mutt's paws.

Once Samson's feet were dry, and Connor's pants were relatively mud free, he brought the puppy in the house and set him in front of his dish.

He dove in snout-first, all but inhaling the food.

Shaking his head at the little glutton, Connor went to wash his hands, then stopped as he caught sight of the table off to his left. "I only count three place settings."

"That's right." Hands full with a bubbling casserole, Olivia glanced over her shoulder. "One for each family member."

"Aren't you eating with us?"

Setting the dish down on a hot pad, she turned to face him directly. "Does Carlotta eat with you?"

"No."

"Then I'm not eating with you, either."

Probably for the best. Yet her response didn't sit well with him. She'd worked hard making dinner for him and the girls, without being asked. The gesture had been a kind one, a thoughtful one. She should enjoy the spoils of her efforts. "Carlotta doesn't eat with us because she prefers to dine with her husband in the evenings."

"I see."

Did she?

Apparently not.

He was going to have to be more specific. "Join us for dinner, Olivia."

He waited for her response. When she simply stared at him, he wondered if she had another commitment. His shoulders bunched at the thought, but again, he couldn't explain the odd reaction. "Unless you have other plans?"

"No." She gave a short laugh. "No plans."

The knot forming between his shoulder blades released. "Then it's settled."

They smiled at each other, neither moving, neither speaking. For a single heartbeat, Connor allowed himself to stare at her, to see her as a woman separate from his friend's kid sister. Strangely drawn to her, he reached out, but then dropped his hand as old loyalties tugged and twisted inside him.

The air between them grew thick with tension, and something else, something that went beyond words. A silent promise of things Connor had long ago forgotten to hope for?

Stunned by the direction of his thoughts, he transferred his weight from one foot to the other.

Olivia shifted to her left.

They broke eye contact simultaneously.

"I'll put the drinks on the table," she said, hurrying around him.

The odd moment was gone. Nothing but a memory now, and Connor couldn't have been more relieved.

Dinner turned out to be far more relaxed than Olivia had expected, especially given the earlier strain between her and Connor. The awkwardness between them made an odd sort of sense. Although they shared a history and their families had been friends for generations, they were veritable strangers.

Determined to keep the mood light, Olivia told stories about her life in Florida. She skimmed over the part about her job loss and breakup with her boyfriend. Instead, she focused on what she did when she had a rare day off.

"I lived in Atlantic Beach, a small town just east of Jacksonville. My house was one block from the beach, so I spent a lot of time there."

"We've never seen the ocean," Megan said on a sigh. Molly agreed with a solemn head bob, then asked, "Can you surf?"

Olivia laughed. "Very poorly, but I can boogie-board."

"What's that?" the girls asked at the same time.

"A much simpler way to catch a wave. You lie flat on a short, foam slab and ride along on your belly. It's sort of like…" she searched for a Colorado equivalent. "…sledding."

"Fun."

"Very."

"All right, girls, that's enough questions for one night." Picking up the near-empty casserole dish, Connor stood. "Time to clear the table and load the dishwasher."

Olivia hopped to her feet and reached for the dish in Connor's hand. "Allow me."

"Absolutely not." Connor held up a hand to ward off an argument. "You cooked. We clean."

"That's the rule in the Mitchell household," Molly told her, sounding very grown up.

"Well, then, I guess that means I'm through for the day."

There was an awkward moment when everyone looked at everyone else.

Then Megan hustled over to Olivia's side. "You're not leaving already, are you?"

She smoothed a hand over the girl's hair, affection swirling in her heart. "Not to worry, sweetie. I'll be back first thing in the morning."

"But you can't go yet. It's Wednesday."

"What's so special about Wednesday?" She aimed the question at Connor.

"Movie night," he explained, heading toward the sink, his hands full of more dirty dishes.

"It's my turn to pick the movie," Molly declared. "And Daddy's turn to make the snacks. He always goes with microwave popcorn. It's a tradition."

Tradition. What a lovely word, one that told Olivia a lot about the man stacking dishes in the sink. She knew the kind of hours he worked, knew the challenges of his schedule even on a "slow" day. Yet he managed a weekly movie night with his daughters.

Could Connor Mitchell get any more likable?

"Well?" Molly demanded. "Are you watching the movie with us or not?"

Tempting. But Olivia didn't want to interject herself into valuable family time. "Maybe next week."

"Olivia." Connor came back to the table, gathered up a handful of silverware. "You're welcome to stay."

She studied his face, noted the sincerity in his eyes. "I don't want to intrude—"

"Stay," he repeated. "Watch the movie with us. Afterward we can discuss your job duties."

They could do that now, before he settled in with the girls, but Olivia didn't point that out. She actually wanted to spend more time with this family, wanted to get to know them on a deeper level.

Dangerous territory.

Or was it? How could she know how best to serve the girls beyond the day-to-day basics if she didn't spend quality time with them?

"All right." She laughed when the girls cheered. "But you have to let me help with the snacks."

"Not going to happen." Connor pointed her toward the family room. "It's my job tonight."

Molly chose a full-length cartoon about a Scottish warrior princess. The snack was, as predicted, microwave popcorn.

Sharing a bowl with Connor, Olivia realized she missed the simply enjoyment of a movie night with people she cared about. She hadn't had a relaxing evening like this since...the night before she broke things off with Warner.

He'd accused her of not wanting a traditional lifestyle. Olivia hadn't disagreed with his accusation. Not because he was right. On the contrary, she desperately wanted marriage and a family of her own. What she didn't want was marriage to a man who considered her a perfect match for his rigid requirements of a wife.

Warner hadn't loved Olivia. He hadn't even wanted her in his life, not really. He'd only wanted a woman who would take care of his daughter on his court-ordered visitation weekends, a woman who had a career worthy of his respect and who, according to him, also looked good on his arm.

Olivia had measured up, supposedly, but she knew any number of women would have taken her place in a heartbeat.

Never again would she be a convenient addition to a man's life. If she married, it would be to a man who loved her for her, not because she exemplified his ideal of the perfect wife.

Hence her desire to focus on her own future and to switch careers before it was too late. Before she woke up and found herself staring down forty instead of thirty, with nothing to show for her life but a VP position at some bank.

And that was enough deep thinking for one night.

"You know what would make this movie even better?" she whispered to Connor, popping a very plain, very bland piece of popcorn into her mouth.

Angling closer, his eyes still on the screen, he lowered his voice to match hers. "What's that?"

"Chocolate."

Chuckling softly, he turned to look at her. His expression was relaxed, approachable, the man behind the successful doctor and stressed-out single dad. "I've always argued that the FDA missed two important food groups."

Smiling like that, almost playfully, made Olivia think of the days when he'd been more boy than man and the center of a few teenage dreams. He'd grown more attractive through the years. He was so good-looking now, so masculine, so *close*. "Wha—what did they miss?"

"Chocolate and coffee. Both deserve their own category. For obvious reasons."

"I like the way you think, Dr. Mitchell."

He chuckled. "And I like—"

"Shhhhhh," Molly ordered. "Here comes the best part."

The best part consisted of an archery tournament

where the female heroine outshone all the men. The kid had excellent taste.

After the movie, Connor sent the girls off to brush their teeth and get ready for bed while Olivia gathered up the empty bowls.

"Can you hang around until I get the twins in bed?"

She lifted a questioning gaze. "Because?"

"We need to discuss your hours, job duties and payment."

"Sure, I can stay a little longer. Why don't I take the puppy for a walk and you can join us outside when you're done getting the girls settled in for the night?"

"It's a plan." With a final smile in her direction, he followed after his daughters.

When Olivia snapped the leash on Samson's collar, he only struggled a little. Vast improvement.

Outside, she breathed in the fresh Colorado air. The scent of pine was heavy tonight. The light breeze lifting the hair off her face carried a slight chill. A refreshing change from the Florida heat and oppressive humidity.

With the sound of clicking bugs and croaking frogs in her ears, she guided the puppy along a grassy pathway bordering a small pond. The sky overhead was dotted with sparkling diamonds against the inky fabric of the night. "Beautiful," she whispered.

The back door creaked on its hinges mere seconds before Connor came up behind her.

"I missed the Colorado nights," she said, her gaze still lifted to the sky. "But I didn't realize how much until I came home."

"I know what you mean." His fingers brushed lightly over hers as he took Samson's leash. "When I was in medical school I couldn't wait to return."

"You attended Tulane, right? In New Orleans?"

"That's right." He looked out across the pond, his gaze as distant as the lone, soulful coyote cry weaving through the night air. "Hottest summers on the planet."

"Florida was equally miserable."

They walked in companionable silence for a while, both lost in their own thoughts. "Connor—"

"Olivia—" he began at the same time.

They laughed awkwardly.

"You first," she said.

He stopped walking, turned to face her. "The girls made sure I knew they had a good day today and asked how long you're staying with us. I told them until Carlotta's knee healed."

Olivia liked the sound of that. "Your daughters are amazing."

"I think so."

His candid response dragged another laugh out of her, the sound far less uneasy than before. "What time do you want me to come back in the morning?"

"Eight too early?"

Her days at the bank had started before seven. "Easy."

They hashed out the rest of the details of her employment as they wound their way around the pond. Connor added, "Ethan and I alternate the extended evening and weekend hours. I'll need you to cover for me here when it's my turn at the office."

"That'll be fine. I'll put a calendar in the kitchen so you can mark the appropriate days to avoid any confusion."

"Good idea."

They fell into a companionable silence and resumed walking.

Samson, the little dear, was behaving for a change. Almost like a regular dog.

When they came full circle, Olivia stopped and stared up at Connor's house. Even in the muted moonlight, the large, three-story structure cut a magnificent picture. The Rocky Mountains, almost purple against the moonlit sky, created a perfect backdrop. "I can't believe you bought Charity House."

"She's a grand old girl, isn't she?"

"What a perfect description."

Connor bent over and picked up the puppy. The little guy looked tuckered out.

So did the big guy.

The strain of the day showed on Connor's face. Tiny lines of tension etched around his mouth and eyes. As it had in the park yesterday, the need to soothe came fast, stronger than before, and nearly impossible to ignore.

She balled her hands into fists, set them on her hips, dropped them by her sides. Sighed.

Who knew simple hand placement could cause such internal conflict?

"The girls are growing up so fast," Connor said, his voice as tired as he looked. "I bought Charity House last year as a way to connect with my family's past while building on the future. I'd like to think we'll add our own stories to the Mitchell lore as time passes."

Merging past and present, forging ahead into the future. What a lovely idea.

"I've always had a thing for this old place." She kept her gaze riveted on the house, afraid if she looked at Connor she might do something foolish. Such as tell him how much she already admired him, respected him.

Liked him.

Guard your heart, Olivia.

"How long have you and the girls lived here?" she asked, banishing all thoughts of the man, save the fact that he was her employer now.

"Barely three months. I started hosting the Mitchell Sunday dinners a few weeks ago. I plan to throw periodic barbecues once the renovations are complete and maybe other parties throughout the year, especially around the holidays."

"That sounds really great."

He lifted a shoulder. "Now that my folks live in Arizona year-round, it's up to me to carry on the Mitchell traditions."

There was that word again. Most of the Scott traditions had died with her parents. And wasn't that the biggest tragedy of all?

Maybe Olivia should follow Connor's lead and restore some of her own family's past while building on the future. *Make a plan. Work the plan. Adjust when necessary.* Maybe she should apply the formula to all parts of her life, not just her career.

"The Scotts have a connection to this house, too," she said, mainly to herself.

"That's right, as do the O'Tooles and the Hawkinses."

"And a few others in town, as well," she said, smiling now. "I wrote a paper about Charity House back in high school and learned a lot about the history of the orphanage."

"I'd love to hear more."

"I'll tell you what I know if you'll give me a tour of the upstairs someday."

"You haven't gone up there yet?"

"I didn't want to roam around your home without your permission, not even with the girls."

He opened his mouth to say something, seemed to reconsider, then began again. "It's getting late. How about I give you that tour tomorrow night when I get home from work?"

"I'd like that very much."

He continued to stare at her, searching her face, saying nothing. "Since it's Ethan's turn to cover the evening hours this week, I should be able to make it home on time."

"That would be nice. But, Connor." She touched his arm, held on a beat. "Remember who you're talking to. I'm the proud granddaughter, daughter and sister of doctors. I'm not going to freak out if you don't show up by six."

The words sounded like a vow, even to her own ears.

His nod was quick, almost imperceptible, but his slow exhale was easily heard. "I'll pay you time and a half if I ever run late."

"That's not necessary."

"Olivia. I have an idea what you were making at the bank in Florida. I'm thinking it was at least five times what I'll be paying you to watch the girls."

That was true. But if today was any indication, watching Megan and Molly was going to be more fun than work. With the bonus of a fully equipped kitchen at her fingertips.

Samson, on the other hand...

An idea struck her, a rather brilliant idea, a colossal win-win. "If it's okay with you, I'd like to bring Baloo with me during the day."

"Any particular reason why?"

"He could use the company and the daily exercise. Who knows, Samson might even pick up a few good manners from the older dog."

"Olivia Scott, you're a genius."

Chapter Six

With Baloo riding shotgun, Olivia arrived at Connor's house fifteen minutes before eight. She told herself she was early because she hated running late. It was not because she was eager to begin watching Molly and Megan full-time. Except…

She *was* eager.

She was getting paid to babysit two adorable girls who happened to live in her favorite house in town. A house fully equipped with state-of-the-art kitchen appliances.

As if he'd heard her approach, Connor appeared on the porch just as Olivia climbed out of her car. The girls joined him a half second later, looking fresh and ready for the day in purple capri pants, matching white T-shirts and identical ponytails.

Olivia's heart sighed as she looked at the twins, especially when she noted how their faces were full of an excitement that matched her own.

"We've been up for hours," Molly said, bouncing in place.

"Hours and hours," Megan added.

An exaggeration, surely. Nevertheless, Olivia smiled in pleasure. She was completely and utterly doomed. After barely a day in the twins' company, her affection for them was quickly outdistancing her need to guard her heart.

Why, oh why, had she put herself in this position to be hurt again?

Simple. This family needed her.

Who didn't like being needed?

She turned her attention to Connor. Bad idea. Legs splayed, hands clasped behind his back, he looked like the essence of a storybook hero, especially with Charity House as his backdrop. Made her think of a lawman taming the Old West.

Oh, no.

She was not interested in this man, she told herself firmly. She was only here to help him out temporarily.

"You're early." He spoke with a smile in his voice, his eyes hidden in the shadows cast by the house behind him.

"I'm a punctual girl by nature." Proud of her own breezy tone, she scrambled around the car and let Baloo out.

"Heel," she told the dog, wanting the shield between her and the family watching her from the porch.

Just when she had her composure back, Connor went and made matters worse. He moved out of the shadows and smiled. Directly at her.

Her pulse fluttered.

Oh, perfect, another visceral response to the man, when she was trying so very, very hard to keep her priorities straight in her head. Connor really was too handsome for his own good.

Baloo let out a happy bark. From inside the house, Samson responded with an exited yip, yip, yip.

"Go on," she told the dog, confirming the command with the accompanying hand signal Ethan had taught her.

Baloo ran up the steps faster than usual and met the puppy in the middle of the foyer. He lowered to his haunches. The smaller dog climbed on his back and began an enthusiastic wrestling match, most of the effort on his end.

Without the buffer between her and the Mitchells, Olivia's heart beat faster, tripping over itself. Stupid heart.

She drew her bottom lip between her teeth, waited for one of them—any of them—to break the silence.

Thankfully, Connor did the honors as he stepped off the porch and joined her on the gravel drive.

"I forgot to give you my cell phone number last night." At her raised eyebrow, he added, "In case you need to get in touch with me and can't get through at the office."

"You should probably have mine, too."

They each typed the other's digits into their respective phones.

"I also forgot to tell you that the microwave can be touchy. If it gets stuck, you have to open the door and start all over again."

She already knew this, but simply smiled and said, "I'm sure I'll figure it out."

He continued as though she hadn't spoken, explaining how to work the thermostat—something she also already knew—the precise location of the garden hose out back and where the washer and dryer were situated in the mudroom. He finished with a detailed rundown on how often to feed the puppy.

Olivia listened, nodding at all the proper places. When he finally took a breath, she placed a hand on his arm. "Go to work, Connor. I've got this. Your girls will be fine in my care."

Smiling her prettiest smile, the one she reserved for the more nervous CEOs, she shooed him toward his car. "We'll see you when you get home tonight."

She took Connor's place on the porch between his daughters. When his taillights disappeared, she stepped back and smiled down at Molly first, then Megan. "Have you had breakfast?"

"Not yet."

"Then we better get to it." She ushered the girls and the dogs inside the house, then directed the whole crew into the kitchen. "Who wants to learn how to make a frittata?"

"Me," the twins said in unison.

"Awesome. We're going to need eggs."

"We always have eggs in the house," Megan supplied helpfully. "Carlotta makes sure of it."

"Okay, then." Olivia opened the refrigerator. "Now. Here. You're officially in charge of these." She handed the egg carton to Molly. "And you hold this." She put a package of cheese in Megan's care. "I'll take the tomatoes. And, oh, good, you have thick-cut bacon. The perfect finishing touch."

Arms full, she shut the refrigerator door with her hip, then went in search of a nonstick pan and a chopping board. Once all the ingredients were laid out before them, she began the girls' second cooking lesson in so many days.

"Natural ingredients are always best."

"That's what Carlotta says."

Although Olivia had never met the housekeeper, she liked her already.

For the next twenty minutes, she patiently walked the girls through the steps of making their first frittata. After they'd eaten and cleaned up, Molly wanted to know what was next on the agenda.

Olivia considered their options. They could go swimming at the local pool, but she'd have to run that by Connor first. She'd do that later tonight. In the meantime, she'd have to figure something else out for them to do.

As she was tapping a finger to her chin, her gaze

landed on Megan's ponytail. *Of course.* "What do you say we have our very own glitter party?"

Megan's eyes popped wide. "What's that?"

"Something I made up back in high school. We practice different hairstyles on one another, paint each other's toenails in sparkly colors, try on various lip glosses and—"

"I'm in," Molly declared before Olivia could finish.

"Me, too."

Olivia smiled at them both. "Then it's settled."

Out of the corner of her eye, she caught Samson sniffing the kitchen floor. He turned in two tight circles.

"Samson, no." She hustled the puppy outside.

The girls chased after her, apologizing for him as they'd done every time he made a mess in the house.

"No worries." She set the animal on the ground. "He's still a puppy. We'll house-train him before long. Let's get him good and worn out so we can leave him in his crate when we head into town to buy all the items we'll need for our glitter party."

Two hours later, Olivia and the girls—plus one very grateful Baloo—sauntered down Main Street. The older dog had had enough of Samson for one morning.

"Olivia Scott, you have some nerve." The teasing words came from behind her. "Instead of stopping in to see me yourself, I have to hear through the town grapevine that you're back home?"

Olivia spun around. "Keely O'Toole!"

"The one and only."

Retracing her steps, Olivia hurried toward her best friend from high school. The ginger hair had deepened to a ruby red, and her porcelain skin radiated around a pair of light green, almond-shaped eyes. Add in that tall, lithe figure and Keely could rival any supermodel in the business.

For a while, she'd done just that.

"I didn't know you were back in Village Green, too." Olivia managed to push the words past her shocked surprise. "I thought you were living in New York."

A shadow fell over the woman's face. "Turns out life in the big city isn't for me."

"Since when?"

"Since I realized how much I missed Village Green."

"This from the girl who couldn't get out of town fast enough?"

"What can I say?" Keely reached down and scratched Baloo's head. "My dreams have changed over the years."

Olivia understood. "How long have you been home?"

"About a year. And I hear you've been back for nearly a week."

"Five days, actually."

"Still too long without stopping in to see me."

Keely wagged a finger at Olivia, her eyes full of amusement. "What kind of friend are you, anyway?"

"The very worst kind. Keely." She pulled her friend into a hug. "It's so good to see you."

They clung, each drinking in the moment, the years slipping away with every second that passed. Keely drew away first, then caught sight of the girls. "Hey, Megan. Molly. What's up, girly-girls?"

"Hey, Miss Keely." Molly hugged the woman, her ponytail swishing back and forth with the gesture. "We're getting ready to have our very own glitter party."

"My very most favorite kind of party ever."

"Mine, too," Megan declared. "Or it will be once I have one."

Keely laughed. So did both girls.

Olivia divided a look between the three of them. They seemed very familiar with one another.

"Well, now that you're here, why don't you come inside for some sustenance before the big party?" Keely gestured at the neighborhood grill her family had owned for generations. Señor O'Toole's. Named after her Irish grandfather and Mexican grandmother. "I'll buy you all lunch."

"Oh, please, Miss Olivia." Megan tugged on her hand. "Can we eat here?"

"I should probably check with your father first."

"It's okay with Daddy," Molly assured her. "He takes us here at least twice a week, sometimes more."

And that, she decided, explained how Keely and

the girls knew one another. As much as she'd love catching up with her friend, she had to decline. "Sorry, we can't. We have Baloo with us."

"No problem." Keely took the dog's leash from Olivia. "We'll sit on the patio out back."

"You have a patio?" That was new.

"Come and see." Keely guided their tiny group around the building, then pointed them to a table beneath a trellis covered in wisteria.

As they settled in wrought-iron chairs, Olivia looked around. The patio was actually a three-tiered terrace. Tables and chairs were scattered beneath festive, multicolored umbrellas that spoke of the family's Mexican heritage, while the dark wood and cobblestone flooring had a definite Irish feel. "I like what you've done with the place."

"Can't take all the credit." Keely poured water from a pitcher into a bowl and set it beside Baloo. "I created the design, but my brother Beau did most of the work."

"I like Beau," Megan said. "He's supernice."

"You know Keely's brother?"

"He taught us how to ski last year." Her face scrunched in a frown. "But I fell a lot."

"Me, too," Molly chimed in. "Beau was really nice, though. He kept telling us that falling was all part of the experience, and if we kept at it we'd be pros in no time."

That sounded like Beau. Keely's twin brother might be one of the baddest, fastest downhill skiers in the world, but he'd always been patient with kids, even back in high school.

"When did he have time to teach you how to ski?" She turned to Keely. "And help you with this patio? Isn't he on the pro tour?"

"Not anymore. Shoulder injury took him out last year."

"I'm sorry. I didn't know." Another reminder of how out of touch Olivia had gotten. Why hadn't she come home more often, or at least tried to stay in contact with friends?

Because she'd been too busy chasing a life that hadn't been meant for her. Even with Warner and Kenzie, there had been something missing, something that left her empty, though she was only realizing that now.

"The accident happened about a month after I came home." Keely grimaced. "When it became evident he wasn't going to make a full recovery, Beau traded one dream for another—his words, not mine—and opened a ski shop in town."

Olivia nodded. "Lemonade out of lemons."

"That's my brother for you. His optimism inspired me to make a few changes other than the terrace." Keely passed her a menu. "Take a look."

Olivia ran her gaze across the items listed.

"Speaking of dreams, whatever happened to yours, Olivia? I thought the plan was for you to get a business degree, then come home and open a tearoom in town specializing in chocolate."

"That's still the plan," she said, setting the menu on the table. She didn't say more, couldn't. She didn't even have a business proposal yet.

But she would. Soon. Very soon.

Make a plan. Work the plan. Adjust when necessary. She really needed to get to that.

Keely motioned over a waitress and ordered the house specialty—shepherd's pie with a Mexican flare—then poured out four glasses of lemonade. "In honor of Beau."

Olivia lifted her glass. "I'll drink to that."

"So." Keely rested her elbows on the table, leaned forward and addressed the girls directly. "How's this one working out as your nanny?" She cocked her head toward Olivia, her green eyes twinkling with good humor.

"We *love* her," Megan said.

Molly agreed with equal enthusiasm. They took turns telling Keely all the reasons why. Olivia's heart whooped and hollered at their sweet words of praise.

Then reality set it.

Kenzie had been equally happy in her care. Looking back, Olivia realized she'd allowed her affection for the girl to influence her feelings for Warner.

Why had she done that? Why had she let herself believe they were a good fit for each other when they'd had so little in common?

He'd been a well-known architect, she a banker. He liked going out and being seen around town.

She'd preferred more quiet evenings at home. He hadn't been a bad man, just not the man for her.

Had she ever really loved him? Or had she only been in love with the idea of a family with him?

Her troubling thoughts were interrupted by the waitress delivering their food. As soon as the girl left, Olivia quickly filled the silence before her mind could return to the past.

"Tell us about your time in New York, Keely. Was it everything you hoped for?"

"And then some." Her words sounded sincere, but her smile didn't quite meet her eyes. "Let's talk about something else besides boring me. I'll start the ball rolling. So, Olivia." She grinned. "Who does your hair?"

"Oh, Keely." Olivia reached out and squeezed her friend's hand. "I've really missed you."

Connor couldn't remember the last time he'd arrived at the office on time. Olivia deserved most of the credit for his smooth transition from home to work. She clearly knew her way around eight-year-old little girls and one overly rambunctious puppy.

She handled big dogs just as well. A single command from her and Baloo had politely trotted onto the porch. The Lab's obedience gave Connor hope that the older dog would, indeed, be a good influence on Samson.

He'd hoped to end the day as smoothly as it started. No such luck. Thanks to a rush of stomach flu cases and a teenager who'd pierced her own nose with disastrous results, Connor didn't steer his SUV out of the office building's parking lot until nearly eight that night.

Not typical, but not unusual, either.

Maybe he and Ethan should consider hiring another doctor.

Twenty minutes later Connor turned onto the gravel drive leading to his house. Golden light beckoned from the downstairs windows, guiding him down the path like a warm promise of better days ahead. An unexpected wave of peace sliced through his exhaustion.

Smiling for the first time in hours, he parked his car next to Olivia's and got out. Childish laughter drifted on the night air. His favorite sound in the world.

Megan and Molly were the heart of him, the best thing he'd done in his thirty-four years of life. In the early days after Sheila's death, when Connor had ached with unspeakable loneliness and grief, the twins had been one of the reasons he'd dragged himself out of bed every morning. Often the only reason.

For four years, he'd put them first, traveling through life with their well-being his main priority. One day at a time. One step at a time.

One problem at a time.

He was ready to do more than just go through

the motions. Not only for the girls' sake, but for his, as well.

No denying the twins needed a woman in their lives, someone to ease them into their teenage years. But Connor thought maybe he needed someone, too. Someone to love and share the burdens of the day, to fill his life with laughter instead of mourning, joy instead of sorrow. Someone who—

He shook away the rest of the thought. With his hours and responsibilities, there was no real opportunity to find a woman to love. Besides, his free time belonged to his daughters.

The moment he entered the foyer, a blast of pop music hit him so hard he nearly fell back a step. He tried to gather his bearings, then noticed the other occupant in the entryway.

Ethan's black Lab eyed Connor fixedly, his big brown eyes filled with a silent plea, as if to say, "Save me."

"Had enough, have you?"

Baloo whimpered.

Pocketing his keys, Connor patted the dog's head, drew in a sharp breath, then went in search of his daughters and their new nanny. He followed the music, winding his way through the house.

Sticking close, Baloo kept even pace with him.

The deeper man and dog moved through the house, the louder the music got.

The music reached an earsplitting crescendo. Female off-key singing joined in the chorus.

He had a bad feeling about what awaited him around the corner. "A *very* bad feeling," he told Baloo.

Bracing for impact, Connor rounded the final turn.

He closed his eyes, opened them again. Winced. A girl bomb had exploded in his home. No other explanation came to mind for the destruction of a perfectly good living room.

Someone had draped blankets in varying shades of pink, pink and more pink across every available piece of furniture. Bottles, jars and tubes of indeterminate girl gunk spotted tabletops. There were a lot of sparkly...things everywhere.

Even the puppy hadn't made it through the day without being dragged into the female whirlwind. Someone had painted the poor dog's toenails in—Connor narrowed his eyes—pink.

On a male dog?

Not sure if he felt a laugh bubbling up, or a groan, Connor zeroed in on his daughters. They had their backs to him, their hair twisted in one of those intricate braids that required a female chromosome to create. Their fingers and toes matched Samson's.

He took several deep breaths and stepped into the room. "I'm home."

Chapter Seven

Olivia looked up. And straight into Connor's stunned gaze. Good thing she was sitting down. Their eyes connected with a force that nearly flattened her.

Her hand flew instinctively to her throat and she thought her heart might be beating far too fast against her rib cage.

A moment of chaos ensued as the twins jumped up and greeted their father.

"We're having our very own glitter party," Molly informed him.

"I…" he circled his gaze around the room "…see that."

"A glitter party!" Megan said with a mixture of wonder and awe. "Seriously. How cool is that?"

"Uh…" Connor blinked several times "…very cool?"

"I know!"

Despite the girls' endless chatter, Samson, still

tucked against Olivia's leg, remained on his back, happily snoring away.

He'd had a busy day.

Olivia rubbed the dog's belly. Then, with eyes still on Connor's stunned face, she rose, steadying herself with a deep inhale.

He's just a man, Olivia. One you've known all your life. It bothered her that she had to keep reminding herself of that, bothered her even more that she hadn't heard the front door open, announcing his arrival. Then again, the music was a bit loud.

She reached over and cut the volume.

Smiling down at his daughters, Connor asked thoughtful questions about their day. They took turns telling him what they'd done. As he listened, he pulled them tightly against him, one on either side. The simple gesture made the three of them a single unit, the very essence of family.

A sigh slipped past Olivia's lips.

She'd already discovered that Connor was a dedicated father, a family man through and through. But she hadn't realized how much she enjoyed watching him interact with his girls.

Her stomach twisted when Connor threw his head back and laughed at Molly's description of Samson's fierce battle with a butterfly this afternoon.

"Who won?" he asked, lips still lifted at the edges.

"The butterfly."

He laughed again, the gesture releasing the majority of the stress in his eyes. The lines around his mouth also softened.

Feeling like an intruder, Olivia looked away from all that family bonding and swiped surreptitiously at her eyes. Warner might not have loved Olivia, but much like Connor, he'd fiercely adored his daughter.

Evidently, she was a sucker for single dads.

Needing something to do with her hands, she organized the bottles of nail polish and tubes of lip gloss in the shoe box Molly had found for her earlier.

"Daddy?" Megan pulled on his arm. "Want to know what?"

"What?"

"Miss Olivia says Molly and I were put on this earth to bring joy and sunshine into your life."

"Miss Olivia is a very wise woman." He winked at her. "You bring joy and sunshine into my life every day."

Olivia's breath caught in her throat.

The quick surge of longing was a reminder of all she was missing in her life. For too long, she'd kept her head down and her mind focused, moving up the corporate ladder fast and furiously. Deep down, she'd known a job couldn't hug her back, couldn't give her a family of her own.

She'd meant to change that with Warner. But he'd only had Kenzie every other weekend. Olivia hadn't needed to adjust her life very much to include either of them. So she'd focused on her career and built time in her schedule for Warner and Kenzie as needed.

She had nothing to show for her efforts. No job. No boyfriend. No family or children of her own. At twenty-nine, she was starting over.

That didn't have to be a bad thing.

Connor kissed both girls on the head and then set them away from him. His eyes narrowed over their faces. "Are you wearing makeup?"

Uh-oh.

"It's just tinted lip gloss," Olivia assured him quickly, setting down the box of bottles and tubes. "Comes off with soap and water."

Molly's shiny lips twisted into a pout. "You don't like how we look?"

"I...think..." He paused, flicked a glance at Olivia, then considered Molly more carefully. "You look beautiful." His gaze included Megan. "Both of you."

They beamed in response and the mood in the room instantly lightened.

Talking over each other, the girls told their father about their trip to the drugstore to pick out their own lip gloss and matching nail polish. He nodded and smiled and actually looked interested in what they had to say.

He also looked tired. His rumpled blond hair and five-o'clock shadow added a bad-boy edge to his otherwise wholesome good looks.

You like him, a voice whispered from deep within her soul.

Yes, she did. She really, really did.

Guard your heart. The Bible verse came quickly to mind. A solid reminder she was only the temporary nanny in this household. Heartache beckoned if she forgot.

"As lovely as you both look," Connor said, a hand on each twin's shoulder, "it's getting late. Time to apply that soap and water, brush your teeth and get ready for bed."

Neither girl argued.

Like Samson, they'd had a busy day, too.

"Will you read to us before we turn out the lights?" Megan asked.

"Oh, please, will you, Daddy?" Molly bounced from one foot to the other. "Will you?"

"I'd like nothing better." He squeezed each of their shoulders. "*After* you wash up and put on your pajamas."

He didn't need to say it twice. They hurried out of the room.

Two seconds later, Molly zoomed back in, Megan hard on her heels. This time, Megan did the talking for them both. "Thank you, Miss Olivia. Today was the best day ever."

"The very best," Molly concurred, launching herself into Olivia's arms.

Olivia pulled the girl close, tears threatening. "Sleep tight." She kissed the blond head, recited the phrase her own mother used to say to her at bedtime. "Don't let the bedbugs bite."

Megan took her turn hugging Olivia before both girls hurried out of the room again, chattering and laughing and, belatedly, calling for Samson.

The exhausted puppy let out a jaw-cracking yawn and rolled over. Blinking the sleep out of his eyes, he hopped to his feet, bobbled a bit, then sped out of the room with his usual enthusiasm.

The little guy was a force of nature, able to hit warp speed in one-point-two seconds flat.

Baloo, not so much.

The older dog lowered to the floor and patently ignored the call to join the girls and Samson.

Rubbing the stubble on his chin, Connor stared after his daughters. The affection in his eyes mirrored the emotion filling Olivia. Despite knowing she needed to keep her heart to herself, she'd already started to care for Megan and Molly. Deeply. They were sweet girls. Smart, creative and, yes, challenging at times. But that only proved they were normal, well-adjusted eight-year-olds.

Before Warner, Olivia hadn't thought much about marriage and children and what the future held for her beyond the next rung up the corporate ladder. She'd been consumed with becoming a VP before turning thirty, content with her chosen path.

Her quick success had seemed a sign from God, a validation that she was right where the Lord wanted her to be. Yet something had been missing. She'd tried to fill the hole with Warner and Kenzie. A mistake. She'd been the one to walk away. But she'd left heartbroken.

"You're good with the girls."

The compliment sent heat crawling toward her cheeks.

She hadn't forgotten Connor was still in the room with her. She just hadn't realized he'd turned around and was now watching her closely. Intently.

What did he see on her face? Longing? Regret? Her wish to do things differently this time around?

"I adore them," she admitted, averting her gaze, steeling her heart. "They're great kids."

"I appreciate you not making a big deal about my late arrival tonight."

She glanced up at the gratitude in his voice. Their eyes met across the short distance between them.

At this close range she could see every nuance of color in his golden eyes, and every unfiltered emotion, a few she didn't recognize or understand. "I can't think of anything I'd rather do than watch your girls this summer."

"I can't think of anyone I'd rather watch them."

He didn't smile as he said the words, yet something pleasant shifted between them, something that went beyond words, something Olivia couldn't quite define.

Maybe she wasn't supposed to try. At least not right now.

"I spoke with Carlotta's husband this afternoon. The surgery went well."

Caught off guard by the abrupt subject change, Olivia took a moment to process the words. "Oh. Oh, Praise God. That's really good news. Answer to prayer."

He blinked at her, looking slightly mystified at her response. "She has a long road to recovery, but she's strong," he said. "With her husband's support she'll get through the rigorous physical therapy just fine."

"I'm glad to hear it."

He broke eye contact, looked around, pressed two fingers against his forehead. "What, exactly, did you do to this room?"

"A little impromptu transformation. I wanted to give the girls a complete experience. And…well…" She tried to take in the room from a man's perspective, cringed as she did. "I suppose I let things get out of hand."

"I don't think I've ever seen so much pink in one room." Lips twisting at a wry angle, he feathered long fingers through his hair. "And that's saying something since I have four younger sisters."

Okay, maybe she'd gone overboard with the whole glitter girl motif. "I should have asked if you had a problem with—"

He cut her off with a laugh. "No apologies necessary. It's cool, Olivia." He picked up a blanket, handed her one end while he kept the other. They folded together in silence.

After a moment, Connor looked around the room again. Winced. "It's really...*pink* in this room."

"Pink is the twins' favorite color." Olivia's, too, which probably explained her slightly defensive tone.

"Not mine," Connor supplied with a grimace. "And, going out on a limb here, I'm pretty sure Samson isn't overly fond of the color, either."

"Point taken. No more painting the puppy's toenails pink."

He lifted a sardonic eyebrow. "How about let's leave the poor animal his dignity and not paint his toenails at all?"

Since he hadn't asked who actually applied the nail polish, Olivia acquiesced quickly. "Done."

They finished folding the blanket, started on another, their movements in perfect rhythm with each other. "You're a good father, Connor."

He paused midfold. "That was certainly out of the blue."

"And yet true." Even though he'd been shocked when he entered the living room, he'd rolled with it, and had even made a point of complimenting his daughters.

"You know, Olivia—" he pulled in a sharp breath of air, then released it along with a slow smile "—I think I needed to hear that tonight."

She liked knowing she'd put that pleased look on his face. Smiling now as well, she took the blanket from him and started folding another, this time without his help.

"Once I get this room cleaned up—" she looked around, noted that the job was nearly complete "—I'll head home. Unless you need me to do something before I go."

"Nothing I can think of."

"Okay." She turned to face him fully.

An inexplicable urge drew her a step closer.

His smile deepened.

"I enjoyed coming home and seeing my daughters having so much fun. Girl fun." He reached for her hand and linked their fingers together with a casualness that spoke of easy camaraderie. Just two old friends reconnecting. "Thank you, Olivia."

"You're welcome."

Silence hung between them, turning slightly awkward. Connor's smile disappeared. And yet he didn't release her hand. The connection felt real, a step toward something new and profound.

Though Olivia knew it was dangerous to do so, she smiled at Connor.

His smile returned.

As if time itself paused just for them, for this moment, they continued staring at each other.

He leaned toward her.

She leaned toward him.

Then... He let go of her hand and took a step back.

"I'll see you in the morning." He attempted to smile again, didn't quite pull it off. "Same time, same place?"

She couldn't think of anything to say to the obvious dismissal. Should she address what had just happened between them?

What would she say? She had no idea what had just happened between them.

"Okay, sure." She gathered her things as quickly as possible, then clipped Baloo's leash into his collar and led the dog into the hallway.

"See you tomorrow, Connor," she said over her shoulder. "Same time, same place."

As far as parting shots went, she could have done worse. Then again, she could have done better.

Olivia had been gone less than five minutes when Connor accepted the truth gnawing at him. He regretted sending her away so abruptly. He'd acted on impulse. The atmosphere between them had been tense, but not that tense.

He'd overreacted and dismissed her with a callousness he hadn't felt.

He needed to apologize.

He had no idea how to broach the subject.

Thankfully, he remembered his promise from the night before, the one he'd inadvertently squelched on by arriving home late. It was the perfect excuse to contact her.

Trying not to think too hard about what he was doing—or why—he pulled out his cell phone, searched through his contacts and punched in her name.

She answered on the fourth ring, sounding breathless and slightly flustered, as if she'd been fumbling to get to her phone before the call went to voice mail.

"Olivia. It's me. Connor."

"Connor?" Her voice took on a worried note. "Is everything all right with the girls?"

"They're fine."

"Okay. Okay, good." Still sounding breathless, she asked, "So. What's up?"

Feeling oddly out of breath himself, he cleared his throat once, twice. Then forged ahead: "I just remembered that I…"

He let his words trail off, unsure why he couldn't continue. This was Olivia. His best friend's kid sister.

Who wasn't a kid anymore.

And that, he realized, was the source of his hesitation. The moment she'd left his house he'd suffered a bout of yearning. For something that went beyond words, beyond logic. And was solely between them.

Guilt roiled in his gut. The sensation was complicated and multilayered on too many levels to explore at the moment. Maybe never.

"Connor? You still there?"

"Still here," he said, gripping the phone tighter. "I just remembered I never gave you your tour."

"What tour?" She sounded bewildered.

He knew the feeling.

"I promised to show you the top two floors of my house."

"Of course. How could I have forgotten?" She laughed, a sweet, feminine sound that spread warmth all the way to the outer edges of his soul. "Guess it'll have to wait until tomorrow."

He wanted to show her around now, right now. After all, they shared a mutual love of Charity House and its colorful history. He'd also like to get her opinion on what to do with some of the rooms upstairs.

All of which could wait until morning, *should* wait until morning. Yet here he was, trying to persuade Olivia to turn around and come back to him. *To the house,* he corrected in his mind.

"I hate making you wait."

"Oh, you know what the Bible says." She sounded overly pleasant, the cheer in voice almost forced. "Blessed are those who wait."

That was a Bible verse? Possibly.

He hadn't explored the Scriptures since Sheila's death. He hadn't stepped inside a church, either.

"Tell you what." He switched the phone to his other ear, as if the move alone could shift his focus. "If you get here earlier than usual in the morning, I'll show you around before I head to the office."

"How early?"

He had her. He could hear it in her voice, in the eagerness she didn't try to hide. Once again, they were in sync, as they'd been when they folded blankets together. "A half hour, maybe forty-five minutes should do it."

"I could make that work."

"Great. It's a date."

Why had he said that? *Just an expression,* he told himself, relaxing his grip around the phone in his hand. Nothing more than a common saying used by millions of people every day.

"Okay, Connor." She pronounced his name inside a shaky whisper. "I'll see you bright and early tomorrow morning. Looking forward to it."

"Me, too."

And, he really was.

Chapter Eight

A half hour after Olivia left for the night, Connor sat in a chair beside Molly's bed and chose a book in the twins' favorite series of historical novels, Meet Samantha, An American Girl, about an orphan being raised by her wealthy grandmother in the early 1900s.

After pulling out the bookmark, Connor picked up reading where he'd left off, just after Samantha had met a new friend, Nellie.

There was no other sound in the house except his voice and Samson's soft, slightly wheezing snore. The dog had curled himself into a ball at the foot of Megan's bed.

Connor never allowed the puppy to sleep in the girls' room overnight, but he didn't mind letting the little guy hang with them before lights out. Samson was, after all, a part of the family.

Family.

For four years that word had included only Connor

and the girls. Now they had Samson, too. The addition had brought unexpected chaos and additional chores for Connor. The puppy also brought the girls' joy. Connor kind of liked him, too. When he was asleep.

Smiling, he reached out and patted the little dog's round belly. Samson snorted in his sleep but didn't awaken. A night breeze fluttered the curtains, bringing fresh air into the room.

Connor continued reading.

He made it through another page before Molly interrupted him. "I really like Miss Olivia."

"Me, too," Megan agreed.

"Do you like her, too, Daddy?"

He looked up from the book and found both girls watching him closely. He tried not to read too much into those wide, eager gazes, even though he knew exactly what they were up to.

"Of course I like her." Something tugged at his heart as he said the words. "She's been a friend of our family for years."

Molly scowled at him. "That's not what I meant."

As he held his daughter's gaze, a rueful affection filled him. He knew Molly was matchmaking, Not very subtly, either. And not for the first time.

"Daddy, you didn't answer Molly's question."

He turned to smile at Megan. "Yes, I did."

"No, you didn't. Not really." Megan let out a very female sigh of frustration. "Do you like Miss Olivia or not?"

It was Connor's turn to sigh. "Yes, I like her."

No use pretending otherwise. Still, discomfort spread through him. Olivia was only with them on a temporary basis. She would leave Village Green eventually. Even if she stayed, he wouldn't pursue her. Not in the way the girls wanted.

Olivia was a career woman.

Sheila had been one, too, or rather, had planned to be before the twins came along. Connor had been in his third year in medical school when they were born, and unable to dedicate much time to their care.

Sheila had been forced to give up her dream job as a cosmetics buyer for a large department store. Over time, she'd grown to resent him for that. Not at first, only when his new practice had taken him away from home for even longer hours than when he'd been in medical school.

Counseling had gotten them past the rift. When they were finally happy again, she'd gotten sick. It had been a terrible blow.

If Connor married again, and that was a big *if,* it would be to a woman who wouldn't have to make sacrifices to be with him and the girls.

"It doesn't matter if I like her or not. Olivia will be leaving us at the end of the summer."

His declaration didn't stop Molly from pinning him down on the Olivia issue. "She's really pretty. Don't you think so?"

"Yes, very." He blew out a slow breath, remembering the way her hair had shone like black silk under the moonlight last evening, and again tonight, with the lights glowing softly in the living room.

There'd been a moment when he caught her looking at him and the girls with a vulnerable expression in her blue, fathomless eyes. Something about that look had urged him to take her hand when they were finally alone. He'd wanted to comfort her, somehow soothe away that look of pain in her eyes. He'd even considered kissing her. For a full nanosecond.

Then he'd come to his senses and stepped back.

"Do you think, maybe, you might ask Miss Olivia out on a date sometime?"

Connor shook his head, only just realizing Molly had been speaking the entire time he'd been remembering Olivia's many fine features in his mind. "No, sweetheart, I won't be asking her out on a date."

"But…" Molly's bottom lip poked out. "Why not?"

"Because she's your nanny."

"So?" Molly held his stare, mutiny in her eyes. She wanted answers. And she wanted them now.

He tried not to sigh again. "No, I'm not going to ask her out on a date while she's taking care of you and your sister. It's not appropriate."

"But—"

"End of discussion."

"But, *Daddy*." Megan picked up the argument where her sister had left off. "Olivia is also your friend, and Dr. Ethan's sister, and she's—"

Having read a passage several times, Connor

recited the words from memory instead of from the book on his lap.

The girls got the message and stopped interrupting him, but not before they gave each other a long look, communicating silently in their own secret-twin way. He knew what that meant. They weren't through pushing Olivia on him.

This wasn't the first time they'd attempted to set him up with a woman. They'd made no secret about wanting him to find them a new mother. He didn't blame them for that. They barely remembered Sheila, and probably only because he showed them pictures of her periodically.

He still missed her, would always miss her, he knew. But her features were beginning to blur in his mind, often disappearing completely without the help of old photos to refresh his memory.

Connor closed his eyes, struggling to bring forth her image now. He didn't want to forget her face, but feared he would eventually.

"Daddy? Did you lose your place in the story?"

"What? Oh. No." He shook his head and focused on the open page. The words danced in a black haze before him.

He recited the next section from memory, glancing up at the girls briefly. Megan's lids were drooping. But Molly stared hard at him. He could practically hear her little mind working overtime, trying to figure out how best to put him and Olivia together.

Molly's tenacity would serve her well in life,

though Connor would prefer her to focus on something more age-appropriate than matchmaking him with women.

She'd introduced him to her teacher a few months ago, with the express purpose of presenting the woman as a potential girlfriend. Then, a few weeks later, she'd suggested he ask out Keely O'Toole.

Connor hadn't felt a single spark for either woman. Or *any* woman the girls had thrown his way. Not one had captured his attention. Until Olivia. He felt something for her. Something strong. Something he immediately shut down.

He found his place in the story and read the next paragraph. Finally, Molly's lids began to droop.

Connor read until both girls drifted off to sleep, which was less than ten minutes later.

Setting the book quietly on the nightstand, he picked up Samson and went in search of the photo album he kept in the dining-room credenza, the one with pictures of Sheila.

The lecture Olivia had given herself on the drive over to Connor's house the next morning was designed to steel her heart against the man's many attractive qualities. So he loved his daughters, and worked hard to put them first in his life. That was not a reason to fall for the man. In fact, it was further reason to keep her distance.

She wouldn't settle for a man who only saw her

as nothing more valuable than his daughters' glorified nanny.

You are his daughters' nanny.

Right. And she had her own plans for the future. She'd spent an hour earlier this morning on her business proposal, determined to remember where her priorities needed to be. Yet Connor's parting words on the phone last night made her pause, consider, wonder. *"It's a date."*

Just an expression, she reminded herself, nothing to take too seriously. She would be gone from his home soon, anyway.

She put the car in park and there he stood, waiting for her on the front porch. Smiling. At her.

Oh, boy.

Olivia hopped out of her car and forced one foot in front of the other. Somehow she managed to let Baloo out of the car and walk up the steps without tripping. "Hi."

Warmth filled his gaze. "Hi."

She waited a beat, but he didn't say anything more.

In the ensuing silence, her heart tumbled to her toes, right along with her composure. It took several quick snatches of air to regain her equilibrium.

Baloo trotted past her, looking around the porch for his little friend.

Connor patted the dog's head. "He's waiting for you in the foyer."

One more pat on the head and he let the black

Lab inside the house, then shut the door behind him with a soft click.

Silence fell over them, broken only by the sound of the dogs greeting each other.

"I…um…" Olivia pulled in a tight breath. "I'm ready for my tour."

"Then come with me." He took her hand and guided her back down the steps to the gravel drive.

Hand resting lightly in his, she glanced around. "Where are the girls?"

"Avery took them out to breakfast."

"Oh." She and Connor were alone? Just the two of them.

It's not a date.

Right. She drew her hand free of his. "Speaking of your sister, she told me she's heading to medical school in August. Isn't she a little behind schedule?"

Avery was only a year younger than Olivia, at least six years older than most first-year med students.

"Technically, yes. She already has a degree in secondary science education, but teaching high school wasn't her thing. So she took the MCATs, aced them and is now going back to medical school." The sound of pride on Connor's voice told its own story.

"Smart, determined girl. I knew I liked her for a reason."

They shared a laugh.

"She's working in the office with me this summer. Today's her first day on the job, hence the celebratory breakfast with the girls."

"What a nice gesture, Connor, very big brotherly of you."

He shrugged. "Family comes first."

Three little words. They said so much about the man.

Something inside Olivia shifted, softened.

"So, about that tour…?"

"Come with me." He led her along the side of the house, steering her around the scaffolding, and then stopped just shy of the back stoop. "We'll start here."

Seeing nothing of interest besides an exterior wall, she angled her head in confusion. "Why here?"

"That spot. Right there. Behind you." He pointed to an area of the house over her right shoulder. "That's where the traveling preacher slammed my ancestor up against the wall."

Intrigued, Olivia peered over her shoulder at the brick and mortar, glanced back at Connor. "I'm not familiar with that story."

"U.S. Marshal Logan Mitchell, my great-great-grandfather, was in love with Megan Goodwin and—"

"The preacher was in love with her, too?"

Connor laughed, the sound easy and relaxed. "No. That particular man of God married a famous stage actress."

"Scandalous."

"At the time, very." He placed his palm on the

building beside her head, his gaze lost in the past. "As the story goes, Logan was several years older than Megan, which caused her guardian all sorts of distress."

"How many years are we talking about?"

"Five."

The same age difference between her and Connor. Had he made the connection?

"Because of the considerable gap in their ages—"

"That's not a *considerable* age gap."

"It is if the woman is only seventeen at the time."

Olivia pressed her lips together in an attempt to keep her thoughts on the matter to herself. "Go on."

"Her guardian objected to Logan's pursuit," Connor continued. "Logan, a stubborn, determined Mitchell to the marrow, wanted Megan for his wife and refused to allow anyone to stand in his way."

Olivia grinned. "Gotta love a man who knows his own mind."

"No argument here. As the story goes, Logan had words with Megan's guardian. One thing led to another and the preacher slammed the poor guy up against the wall." He patted the spot beside Olivia's head. "Right here."

Caught in Connor's gaze, Olivia remained perfectly still. Perfectly. Still. "That doesn't sound very preacherlike."

"Supposedly, he was only trying to get Logan's attention."

"Did it work?"

"Temporarily. Logan lost the battle that day, but he won the war." Connor grinned. "He married Megan five years later."

With him leaning over her like this, Olivia could smell Connor's masculine scent, see the flecks of gold weaving through the other shades of brown in his eyes. She took another slow, steadying breath. "A happy ending."

"With a few speed bumps along the way. They said their vows in a jail cell."

"You're kidding."

"Nope, but it's a long story. I'll tell you the rest another time. Come on." He pushed away from her, offered his hand again. "We'll continue the tour inside."

She pressed her palm against his, felt a jolt of recognition that started somewhere deep in her soul.

She yanked her hand away from his.

Opening the back door, Connor paused, waited until she drew alongside him on the steps. "It's your turn to tell me a story about my home."

"Me?"

"Didn't you say you wrote a paper on Charity House when you were in high school?"

"You remember that?"

"I remember everything you tell me." He led her through the house, toward a large staircase, then rested his forearm on the newel post. "That surprises you?"

"Actually, yes. It does."

"I don't see why." Pushing back, he led the way up the first set of stairs, stopping on the landing so she could catch up with him. "You're a remarkable woman, Olivia. I've always thought so."

"I…" She searched for a response, *any* response, but came up empty. "I simply don't know what to say to that."

"Olivia, I'm sorry." Placing his finger beneath her chin, he applied light pressure until she looked directly into his eyes. "I didn't mean to make you uncomfortable."

"You didn't. I'm just, that is… I had no idea you thought of me at all."

"Oh, I think about you."

"I think about you, too."

"Do you, now?" He touched her cheek, a mere whisper of his fingertip across her skin. The gesture was unbearably sweet, tender even.

Afraid she might blurt out what was in her heart, yet not exactly sure what that might be, she scooted past him and hurried down the hallway.

Something was different about Connor today, more intense.

The shift in him made her strangely happy and breathless, and that was a problem. He came with baggage, and far too much potential for heartache. His schedule alone would make a relationship with him difficult.

Even if he freed up time for a woman, part of his heart would always belong to his wife. As she mulled this over, Olivia decided his devotion was as attractive as the man himself. He understood what it took to make a long-term relationship work. Better than most men.

No denying he'd loved once and had loved well.

But would he ever love again? Or had he given everything he had the first time around?

Was the rest reserved for his daughters?

Warner had been divorced and hadn't been able to love both Kenzie and Olivia.

Stopping at the first door on her right, she took a moment to pull her emotions back under control.

When Connor finally came up beside her, he reached behind her and twisted open the door.

Olivia quickly stepped into the room and glanced around. "What's that on the walls?"

"Come and see." He directed her to the wall on their immediate left. "Megan painted this before she became Logan's wife."

"It's a mural, of a…" Olivia studied the faded image "…children's fairy tale?"

"Look closer." Connor moved in beside her. Shoulder-to-shoulder they studied the paintings in silence.

"It's a depiction of Noah's Ark."

"That's right." He ran a finger over the rows of animals moving two by two toward a large, wood boat.

"And over here…" Connor strode to the next wall on their right "…is the parting of the Red Sea.

Megan painted a different scene on every wall, and in every room on this floor."

"What a wonderful legacy for your family."

"I think so."

Olivia roamed through the room, drinking in the faded murals, marveling as she went. Each scene made her want to return to her innocent youth, where dreams still existed, where every boy wanted to grow up to be a courageous knight and every girl a beautiful princess.

Megan had also written Bible verses along the top edges of the walls. *Let the children come to me, and do not hinder them.* And another one, *Fear not, for I have redeemed you. I have summoned you by name.* And her favorite, *Never will I leave you; never will I forsake you.*

As she read the Scriptures silently to herself, Olivia experienced an overwhelming sense of peace, as if God was wrapping His unconditional love around her.

Over a hundred years ago, Connor's great-great-grandmother had created all of this with a paint-brush, a love for the Lord and a vivid imagination. "They're so real, as if the images are about to walk off the wall."

"I'm contemplating having the murals restored."

"A lovely idea."

"Want to see the other paintings?"

"Absolutely." When they entered the next room Olivia went immediately to the image on her right.

"The walls of Jericho." She ran her finger along a swirl of red paint faded to a light pink. "This must be the cord Rahab hung from her window to alert the Israelite soldiers of her location."

"Megan's mother was a prostitute." Connor touched the wall beside Olivia's hand. "I like to think this story especially mattered to her, maybe even gave her hope that she could break the cycle of sin in her family."

"Her faith shows in her artwork. It's beautiful."

"Breathtaking."

Something in his voice had Olivia glancing up at him. Her stomach knotted at the admiration in his eyes, admiration for her. "Connor?"

His name was a mere whisper on her lips.

"You're so beautiful, Olivia."

He sounded sincere, and maybe caught off guard. Was this moment real?

Or were they both caught up in the romance of the past, of the tale of love that had been found by two people others thought didn't belong together?

Connor stepped slightly back, his eyes not quite meeting Olivia's anymore.

A door slammed in the distance, followed by dogs barking and pounding feet.

Not sure what to say before the others joined them, Olivia stared up at Connor.

He stared down at her.

Neither said a word.

"Olivia." He speared his fingers through his hair,

let out a tight breath. "I... You... You're my daughters' nanny."

They might have had an emotional connection just now, a recognition that went beyond words, but nothing would come of it. Nothing *could* come of it. Their lives were going in two separate directions, only crossing because she was a solution to his temporary child-care problem.

She'd been another man's solution once, and knew what came from reading too much into the situation.

"Olivia," Connor began again. "We need to—"

"Daddy?" Molly's voice came from downstairs. "Miss Olivia? Where are you?"

"Up here," Connor called back, then took Olivia's hands in his. "We'll talk about this later. No, don't scowl at me like that. We *will* discuss what just happened between us."

"Nothing happened."

"You know that's not true."

He let go of her hands and stepped away from her. The twins entered the room a second later with Connor's sister right behind them.

"Wow." Avery's feet ground to a halt. "Look at those walls."

Welcoming the topic of discussion, Olivia smoothed her face free of expression. "They're great, aren't they?"

"Amazing. I haven't been up here yet. I didn't know." Avery stepped deeper into the room, her gaze traveling from one mural to the next. Slowly, she turned her attention back to Olivia and Connor. "Sorry, didn't mean to be rude, got caught up in the gorgeous murals."

"Understandable." Olivia smiled at the other woman, or rather she tried to smile. She was still shaky from the strange encounter with Connor moments before.

Avery's gaze narrowed over her face. She glanced from her brother to Olivia and back again. With each pass, a knowing glint settled in her eyes. "Did we interrupt something?"

Connor and Olivia answered simultaneously, "No."

"All righty, then." Clearly, Avery wasn't buying their response. At least she didn't call them out in front of the twins.

"Ready to go to work, big brother? Assuming you can tear yourself away from your beautiful, compelling…" She paused a beat, looked pointedly at Olivia. *"Artwork."*

Chapter Nine

Several days later, Connor navigated a slow morning in the office by updating patient charts. The beautiful weather beckoned, urging him to play hooky. His mind wanted to wander, back to the moment in his house when he and Olivia had...

What? What, actually, had happened between them?

A shift had occurred in their relationship. But he couldn't put a name to it, didn't want to put a name to it.

He focused on work, opening the next file on his laptop and scanning his incomplete notes.

Halfway through expanding his diagnosis in clearer terms, Ethan stuck his head in the doorway. "Got a minute?"

He pushed back from his desk. "Sure."

Expression bland, Ethan plunked down in one of

the chairs facing Connor's desk. "How's Olivia getting on with the girls?"

"You'd think she'd known them all their lives."

"That good, huh?"

"That good."

"So." Ethan set his feet on the desk, crossed his ankles and went fishing without a pole. "She say anything to you about why she came home?"

"Only that she's between jobs. I didn't ask for more." He'd been too busy trying to keep his distance, avoiding any personal connection.

And not always succeeding.

Probably not the direction his thoughts should be taking with her brother eyeing him with those all-knowing, all-seeing Ranger eyes.

"She's hiding something from me, or rather, withholding key pieces of information," Ethan said, frustration obvious in his tone. "I get the feeling something more than her job loss drove her home."

No, Connor wasn't getting in the middle of this. "Maybe you should ask her directly."

"You think I haven't tried?" He rubbed his chin. "She keeps saying she has…plans and will share them with me when she has something more concrete to present. She supposedly needs more time."

"Then give her more time."

Ethan looked out the window, his gaze seeming to latch on to something in the distance. "She's not in trouble. At least, I don't get that read."

"Maybe your mind-reading skills are off."

Ethan threw him a get-real look. "They're never off."

Right. "Leave it alone, Ethan. Olivia's a grown woman. She'll talk to you when and if she decides you need to know what's going on with her."

"Guess there's not much else I can do but wait her out. And that's not the reason I'm here." He stood, gave Connor a quick once-over. "I came to tell you to take the rest of the day off."

"It's not even noon and I already had my day off this week."

"You covered for me the other night, no questions asked, so…" He dug in his back pocket. "Here's my way of saying thanks."

"We're partners. I don't need thanks. You've done the same for me countless times and I— Are those Bobcats tickets?"

Connor leaned forward, his gaze zeroing in on the logo of Village Green's minor league baseball team. The purple cat snarled at him from just beneath Ethan's thumb.

"Four seats directly behind first base." Ethan handed the tickets across the desk. "Treat your girls to an afternoon of baseball, hot dogs and fun in the sun."

His twins loved baseball. Not as much as Connor did, but they were still young yet. He studied the tickets, noted the game started in two hours. Plenty of time to pick up the girls. He counted out three, then handed back the fourth. "I don't need this one."

"It's for Olivia."

He hadn't thought to bring Olivia, but now that Ethan put the idea in his head...

"She might want the afternoon off."

Ethan shrugged. "Won't know till you ask."

Before he could thank his friend, their nurse, Tasha, entered the office. "Hope I'm not disturbing you two, but Lacy Hargrove's back again. Says she's dizzy and seeing spots." She rolled her eyes.

Ethan headed for the door. "Be right there."

The nurse shared a look with Connor.

Ethan caught them. "What?"

"You're actually volunteering to see Lacy?"

Not quite hiding his grimace, the other doctor lifted a nonchalant shoulder. "It's my turn to take one for the team. And it's your turn—" he pointed at Connor "—to go have fun with your girls."

"Don't have to tell me twice." Giving Ethan no time to change his mind, Connor shut off his computer and gathered his belongings. "I'm out of here."

Fifteen minutes later he nosed his SUV onto Aspen Way. He'd already called Olivia to tell her he had a treat for his girls. *His girls.* It didn't occur to him until he swung onto the gravel drive that somewhere between the office and home he'd begun to include Olivia in that term.

His chest tightened at the thought.

The moment he cut the engine, the front door

opened and the twins rushed out. Olivia caught up a second later, moved in between the girls and slung her arms over their shoulders.

The cinch around his chest clutched tighter.

They looked so right together, standing on the edge of the porch with their arms linked and pretty smiles on their faces. The dogs joined them, one on either side of the twins. As if waiting for this precise moment, the sun split through a seam in the clouds and washed the tiny group in golden light.

Huh.

Connor's soul felt a little less empty as he commandeered the front steps.

"Welcome home, Daddy."

Home. Yes. He was home. With *his girls*.

"Hi." He looked at Olivia as he spoke the greeting.

Her smile widened. "Hi."

Molly shifted into view, her voice a mixture of impatience and little-girl excitement. "Miss Olivia said you have a surprise for us."

"I'm taking you to a Bobcats baseball game."

"Today?"

"Right now."

"Awesome." Molly spun in a delighted circle.

Megan joined in the celebration, skipping around her sister. Samson caught on to the game and proceeded to leap in the air and bark wildly. Polite as always, Baloo remained sitting at attention and looked up at the sky, the equivalent of a canine eye-roll.

"We're leaving in twenty minutes," he told the

twins over the chaos. "Go do whatever little girls do before spending the day at a baseball game."

They hurried off, Samson chasing in their wake.

Olivia stayed behind, hand on Baloo's shoulders.

Aware her eyes were on him, Connor slowly turned his head. He dropped his gaze over her simple shorts and green T-shirt. Even in clothes that could be described as plain and boring, she was the essence of femininity.

Something in him softened. Toward Olivia. Toward—

He cleared his throat.

"You've just made their day," she said, touching his forearm, sliding her fingers down to wrap around his hand a moment.

Such a simple gesture, yet he had a sudden urge to ride off to battle. To slay dragons. To fight the good fight. Something about this woman made him want to step up, to be a better man. To reach for…more.

A movement at his feet caught his attention. Samson had returned, with one of Connor's socks in his mouth. After a few hard tugs, followed by Samson's playful growls, Connor picked up the puppy and held him against his chest.

He knew he was using the animal as a shield between him and Olivia. Couldn't be helped. They'd crossed another line just now, and all she'd done was cover his hand with hers for a few seconds before letting him go.

He dragged his gaze over her face and wondered

why Olivia was the only woman since Sheila who made him want to live beyond the moment, to look toward tomorrow.

"Ethan gave me four tickets to the game. He thought you might like to join us."

"Wouldn't you rather have time alone with your girls?"

He'd definitely like time alone with *his girls*.

"I want you to come with us." He touched her cheek with his knuckle. "Say yes, Olivia."

Her eyes clouded over for a beat. Then her smile returned, brighter than before. "Yes."

The crack of a bat connecting with a slow, dangling slider brought a roar from the crowd. Connor set his soda under his seat just as Olivia lurched to her feet and yelled at the Bobcats' batter to "Go, go, go."

Megan and Molly joined in the chant, jumping up and down, their higher-pitched voices full of excitement.

Connor jumped up, too, cheering with the rest of the fans already on their feet. "Run," he shouted, pumping his fist in the air. *"Run."*

Heart pounding, he glanced at the scoreboard, confirmed the tight situation. Bottom of the eighth. The home team was down by three. He turned back to the game. Bases loaded, with only one out.

The pop fly dropped in the dead zone between

two unprepared outfielders. They scrambled over each other to get to the ball.

The player on third-base headed for home.

Olivia bounced up and down. "He's going to make it. Connor, he's going to score."

"Yeah, he is."

"Safe." The umpire confirmed his ruling with a fast, outward sweep of his arms.

Connor bumped fists with Molly, then Megan.

The third base coach wound his arm in the air, urging the next player to keep on going. And the next one after that.

The second player slid home. "Safe!"

Connor high-fived Olivia. "That's what I'm talking about."

The third runner made his move. But now the opposing team had their bearings back. A split second later the ball whooshed into the catcher's glove.

"Out," yelled the umpire.

Olivia groaned with the rest of the home crowd, a surprisingly large showing for an afternoon game in the middle of the week.

She sank back in her seat. Megan followed, as did Connor.

Molly remained standing, bouncing from foot to foot, eyes squeezed tightly shut. "We're gonna win. We're gonna win. We're gonna win."

"You know it." Olivia clasped her hand and tugged her into the seat beside. "As Yogi Berra always said, it ain't over—"

"Till it's over." Connor finished the famous line with her.

She laughed.

He joined in, feeling light, happy. Relaxed.

For the first time in months, Connor didn't think about work, or the endless responsibilities requiring his immediate attention. He didn't even worry about Samson back home, asleep in his crate. Not much, anyway.

All he thought about was his girls and the woman in the seat next to him, a woman who loved baseball as much as he did. He had a sudden urge to pull her near. For no other reason than he was glad she'd joined them today.

A jolt of alarm followed the thought. Things were getting a little too close for comfort between him and Olivia. She'd wiggled past his defenses and he wasn't sure what to do about it.

Enjoy yourself, came the whispered thought.

Not a bad idea.

"What a beautiful day for a baseball game." She gestured to the lush green outfield, then arced her hand in the air. "Eighty degrees, clear blue skies and, of course—" she winked at him "—stellar company."

He brushed his hand lightly over hers. "Can't ask for more."

"Speak for yourself. I want a win."

"Getting greedy, Miss Scott?"

"Absolutely, Dr. Mitchell." She tapped him playfully on the chest. "Now stop distracting me. I'm trying to watch a very close game."

Molly scooted over to the seat on his other side, wiggled in beside her sister and whispered, "Thanks, Daddy."

"For what?"

She glanced over at Olivia. "For bringing her with us. Today wouldn't be the same without her."

"No, it wouldn't."

"Ha." She gave him a little-girl grin. "I *knew* you liked her."

The next batter moved into position at the plate, then stepped back when the opposing coach called time and jogged out to the pitcher's mound.

Attention riveted on the game, Olivia leaned forward. As she did, her long, silky hair brushed against Connor's arm.

His stomach clenched.

Blinking hard, he focused on the scoreboard, then the outfield, swung his gaze over to the pitcher's mound. His mind refused to settle, kept spinning back to the woman beside him and how her presence brought a sense of calm to his chaotic home, to his life, maybe even to his very soul.

Irritation followed, moving through the sensation like yeast through dough.

Megan moved around her sister and sat on Connor's lap. "Molly ate all the popcorn. Can we get more?"

Actually, Megan had eaten her share, too, but Connor welcomed the distraction. "Sure."

He set her on her feet and stood. "Anyone want to come with me to the concession stand?"

"No way." Megan shook her head adamantly. "I want to stay here with Miss Olivia."

Molly ignored the question completely. She was too busy staring down the opposing coach as he left the pitcher's mound.

"Olivia? That okay with you?"

"Go on, Connor. The girls and I will keep the seats warm." She waved him off with a preoccupied toss of her hand. "Won't we, girls?"

"Yep," Megan said, taking the seat he'd just vacated.

Molly pointed to home plate. "Batter up."

Shaking his head, Connor left for the concession stand on his own. All three of his girls barely noticed his departure. They clasped hands and leaned forward, eyes glued to the game.

With half his mind on the game, he let the other half wander. Before Olivia had returned to Village Green, Connor had been navigating through life just fine, maintaining the status quo. Though there were times when he collapsed in the bed at night, exhausted, he'd been fairly satisfied.

He had the twins. A rewarding career.

And a carefully balanced, ruthlessly ordered life.

Now, thanks to her influence, Connor was aware of an underlying restlessness that had begun to tug at him. The sensation had always been there, he realized, ever since Sheila's illness. Maybe even before?

A traitorous thought.

Yes, he and Sheila had hit a rocky patch before she'd gotten ill. So she'd threatened to leave him if he didn't stop working thirteen-hour days. Connor had rearranged his priorities, taken on Ethan as his partner. He'd even gone to counseling with her, and had prayed for direction. He'd done everything right, remained faithful, putting his hope in the Lord.

To what end? Sheila had died anyway.

Connor took a sip of the soda he'd brought with him, then stared into the cup as if the meaning of life swirled deep inside the dark liquid.

The anger was there, he admitted, riding him hard, urging him to shake his fist at the Lord. But Connor controlled the emotion. Every day, he controlled it, shoved it down, pretended all was well. For his daughters' sake. For Sheila's, too, and the promise he'd made before she died. He would raise the girls in the church, would ensure that they learned *the way they should go*.

No one needed to know what was really in his heart.

Except…

Connor knew.

And the more time passed, the more he wanted freedom from the anger and pain he kept buried deep inside. He wanted a peace that had eluded him for years.

At the front of the line, Connor ordered the popcorn and returned to his seats.

He sat in Megan's empty chair and handed over the bag. "Thanks."

"You're welcome." He concentrated on the game, only the game.

Still two outs, but the bases were loaded once again.

The ball whizzed in the air toward home plate. The batter swung and...*smack*.

Olivia and the girls were back on her feet, screaming at the ball flying through the air. "Get up. Get up, you stupid ball. Up, up, up!"

This time, Connor didn't rise to his feet. He sat back and watched Olivia and the girls cheer on the team.

Their enthusiasm charmed him.

Olivia was a good influence on his daughters. She was so full of life, so uninhibited in her excitement, so throat-cloggingly beautiful. And she loved baseball. If Connor found out she was also a football fan, he'd be in trouble.

You're already there.

Yeah, he was. He was also a guy. So he did what guys did in emotionally charged situations. He ignored the sensation and belatedly rose to his feet just as the ball sailed over the outfield wall.

Home run.

The crowd went wild.

In that moment, Connor stopped thinking about

the past, stopped feeling guilty, stopped wondering what came next.

He exchanged a look with Olivia. A thousand words passed between them. And everything in him settled.

He knew the peace flowing through him wouldn't last. But for now, in this brief instant, he let a sense of calm fill him.

The Bobcats eventually claimed the win seven runs to three. Megan and Molly jumped up and down with the other fans. Olivia and Connor stayed seated, smiling at each other.

Despite the crowd rising, gathering their things, moving around them, Connor didn't want to leave just yet.

He wanted to soak in the moment.

"There." Olivia pointed to the scoreboard. "That's what I call a perfect ending to a wonderful day at the ball field."

"I couldn't agree more." Laughing, Connor pulled his daughters close, continued smiling at Olivia.

He started to speak again, but whatever had been in his mind slipped away. Replaced by another, more disturbing revelation.

He didn't just like Olivia, didn't just value the way she took care of his daughters. He admired her. Respected her. Wanted to get to know her better.

He might even be on the verge of falling for her.

On some level, he realized, he might already be halfway there.

Chapter Ten

Both girls were sound asleep by the time Connor turned his SUV onto the gravel drive leading to his home. Olivia watched him out of the corner of her eye, an uneasy sensation making her shoulders bunch. Ever since leaving the game, she and Connor had fallen into a friendly camaraderie, emphasis on friendly.

At least on the surface.

Under the surface bubbled all sorts of tension, strain and discomfort, a virtual hat trick of complicated emotions.

Something had changed between them, at least on Connor's end. Despite his outward attempt to keep the atmosphere light and friendly in the car, he was more distant than ever before.

Olivia wished she knew what had caused his need to put up a metaphorical wall between them. She thought they'd had a good day. But she'd caught Connor watching her several times, his brows knit together, as if he couldn't quite reconcile her presence in his car, maybe even in his life.

During those uncomfortable moments, hoping to alleviate the awkwardness, she would smile at him. He would smile back. They would have a moment. Similar to the one they'd shared in the upstairs room with all the murals. Then he would turn back to look out the windshield and strike up a benign conversation with one of the girls.

Now, with both Molly and Megan sleeping soundly, he navigated the drive in silence, pulling his SUV in next to her BMW.

He cut the engine and sat back but didn't make a move to get out. She touched his arm, nothing more than a slide of her fingertips along his sleeve, but his muscles tensed.

"Connor." She kept her voice low, not wanting to wake the girls. "Is everything okay?"

He nodded, then slipped out of the car and opened the door behind him. Olivia followed suit, opening the door on her side of the car, as well. She nudged Megan awake, while Connor did the same with Molly.

Megan awakened slowly, blinking up at her. "Are we home?"

"We are."

Yawning loudly, Molly leaned over the center console to speak to Olivia. "Will you read to us tonight?"

The question sent alarm washing through her.

There was something all-too-intimate about reading bedtime stories to a child. It was so...parental. "Aren't you too tired?"

"Please, Miss Olivia?"

The plea in the girl's eyes nearly did her in. How was she supposed to say no to that? She glanced across the top of the car, locked gazes with Connor. "If your father says it's okay."

He lifted a shoulder. "Maybe a page or two, but I doubt they'll last much longer than that."

Olivia wondered if reading to the girls also meant she would get to say prayers with them, too. She figured they would explain their routine once they were upstairs.

The four of them trooped into the house to the accompanying sound of Samson's crazed yips.

Connor instantly changed direction. "I'll take care of the puppy."

"Then I'll head up with the girls."

A quick nod on his part, a soft sigh on hers and they went their separate ways.

By the time the twins were tucked in their bed, their faces washed, teeth brushed and prayers said, Olivia's heart had taken another couple of hits. The twins were genuinely happy to have her part of their evening routine and had said as much at least three times each. Even their prayers had included heartfelt thanks to the Lord for bringing her into their lives.

Eyes wet, her heart shattered into pieces, Olivia accepted the truth. She loved Molly and Megan as if they were her own. It had happened so fast. Not that she'd put up much of a fight.

Sighing, she sat in a chair between their two beds, opened the book in her lap and set aside the bookmark Connor had left on page 37. "Ready?"

Instead of answering her question, two pair of amber-colored eyes stared back at her. They had something on their minds.

"Okay, what's up?"

They looked at each other, exchanged one of their silent twin messages and then turned back to study Olivia with identical expressions of interest.

She waited.

"Did you know our mom?" Molly finally asked her.

The question struck Olivia in the heart like a well-aimed arrow from a master marksman. She'd assumed the twins would eventually ask her this, for the simple reason she'd grown up in Village Green, but Olivia hadn't seen it coming tonight.

Throat tight, she shut the book and took a steadying breath. "I knew her a little. But she was friendlier with my brothers, especially Ethan."

"Because she was Daddy's girlfriend and Dr. Ethan is Daddy's very best friend in the whole world?" Megan suggested.

Smiling at Megan's choice of words, Olivia nodded. "That's partly the reason. But also because she was in the same grade as Ethan. She was five grades ahead of me, so I never actually attended school with her."

"Oh." Molly considered this a moment. "Do you remember if she was pretty?"

Olivia's breath caught at the vulnerable look in the young girl's eyes, but she recovered quickly and answered the question truthfully. "Your mother was one of the most beautiful girls in town. All the boys thought your father was the luckiest guy on the planet."

Molly sighed wistfully. "Daddy says we look like her."

"You do." Olivia moved to sit on the bed beside Molly, took the girl's hand. She reached out and took Megan's, as well. "You two are already as beautiful as she was. The men who win your hearts will be the luckiest guys on the planet, too."

Both girls smiled.

Olivia squeezed their hands gently, praying the gesture offered comfort.

"Daddy shows us pictures of her sometimes." Molly's lower lip quivered. "But I don't really remember her."

"Me, either," Megan said, very softly. "I think it makes Daddy sad when we can't remember her." Tears filled the young girl's eyes.

Olivia swallowed back her own tears. "I'm sure he understands, sweetie. He probably shows you the pictures so you can remember her always."

Both girls nodded.

Megan whispered her name.

"Yes?"

"Do you—" she blinked up at Olivia "—do you like our daddy?"

A keen ache pierced the center of her soul. "Of course I like him. Our families have been friends forever and ever."

"Yeah." Molly sighed heavily. "That's what he said when we asked him the same question."

Oh, boy.

"But then he said he couldn't ask you out on a date because you're our nanny."

"That's true," she rasped, wishing she had a clue how to navigate this conversation better. She was in way over her head. "It's best if we keep our relationship strictly professional."

The girls exchanged another look, their little lips pursed in identical looks of frustration and resolve.

Olivia knew better than to ask what was on their minds. Releasing their hands, she picked up the book and moved back to the chair between their beds.

Both girls leaned back against their pillows and closed their eyes.

Olivia watched them another moment, then lowered her head and started reading at the top of the page.

Connor stood outside the twins' bedroom, listening as Olivia's sweet, lilting voice picked up the story of Samantha and her friend Nellie where he'd left off.

He stayed out of sight and let her voice wash over him.

The story sounded different coming from her. Her inflection was almost comforting, soothing even, and very female.

He peered into the room. His gaze sought and found Olivia. With her head bent, her lips moving, there was a softness about her and her voice was filled with an underlying tenderness, as if she was being very careful with the girls tonight.

The twins looked peaceful in their beds, their eyes closed, little smiles on their faces. His heart tripped over the sight.

Connor tried not to read too much into the situation. Olivia was simply doing her job, nothing more. Yet he couldn't help thinking she was right where she belonged. In his home. Reading to his daughters while he watched over them.

He started at the direction of his thoughts, torn between guilt and satisfaction as he straddled the precarious spot between past and present, old and new.

Olivia paused, looked up, caught him staring.

Her blue-blue eyes searched his, her gaze full of profound gentleness, as if she understood the conflict waging inside him.

He swallowed another wave of unease.

She mercifully looked back to her book.

On surprisingly unsteady legs, Connor quietly left

the hallway. Panic had him searching for the photo album he'd pulled out the other day.

Needing air, he took the book outside and settled on the back stoop. He drew in a deep breath, let it out slowly and opened to a random page. A picture from his and Sheila's honeymoon jumped out at him. They'd been happy, both mugging for the camera on the edge of a sandy beach in the Caribbean.

He studied the image of his wife's smiling face until he had it permanently fixed in his mind. Then closed the album and set it on the ground by his feet.

But as soon as he looked up, the image slipped from his mind. This time, the sensation didn't bring the usual spurt of pain. He even felt a smidgen of peace, as if he was letting her go slowly and it was the right thing to do.

Olivia was partly to blame.

Watching her read to his girls tonight, remembering how well the day had gone with all four of them at the baseball game, gave him hope for the future. Hope that he might actually find another woman to share his life. It wouldn't be Olivia.

Not if she left town to pursue her career.

What if she didn't leave town? Would she be someone he could see in his life?

She was certainly special and had brought calm to his chaotic home. No matter what happened between them, *if* anything happened between them, Connor could never go back to just going through the motions.

Olivia had awakened something in him that couldn't be ignored—a desire to start living again, without grief weighing him down.

Behind him, the door between the kitchen and the mudroom creaked on its hinges. "Connor?"

"Out here," he called. "On the back stoop."

Olivia poked her head out the doorway. "I just wanted to let you know the girls are asleep and I'm heading out now."

Not thinking too hard about what he was doing, or why, he patted the spot beside him. "Sit with me a moment before you go."

"All right." She settled in beside him.

He could feel her eyes on him, could practically hear the questions running around in her head. She had to be wondering why he'd called her outside to sit with him.

He wasn't sure himself.

"I owe my brother a huge thank-you. That was an awesome game."

"Yeah, it was." Not only because the Bobcats won.

He expected her to say more, but she simply looked up at the sky. She reached out and covered his hand with hers.

Her touch should have put him on edge. Instead, he felt the tension drain out of him, inch by agonizing inch. For a dangerous moment, he wanted to tell her how worn out he felt most days, how overwhelmed he was trying to be both father and mother to his daughters.

Would the confession be a betrayal to Sheila?

Or a step toward moving on with his life?

Drawing in a ragged breath, he pulled his hand out from under Olivia's. She turned her head and smiled at him, the look in her eyes full of understanding. "Connor, I was thinking—"

Her cell phone rang, screeching out a popular version of the song "Bad to the Bone." Olivia scowled at the interruption but didn't immediately answer the call.

"Aren't you going to take that?"

"Still debating." The ring tone hit a crescendo. *Baaaaad to the bone.* "It's Ethan."

Ba-ba-ba-baaaaad.

Lips twitching at the very appropriate ring tone, Connor shook his head. "Might as well see what he wants."

"He's probably just wondering where I am."

"Which means he's worried about you."

She made a face. "Why would he be worried about me? I've lived nearly ten years on my own."

"Take the call, Olivia."

Frowning at him, she pressed Talk and then put the phone up to her ear. "Hello?"

Ethan said something Connor couldn't make out.

"Sorry, E. I meant to text you. The game went long." She looked over at Connor. "And then we stopped for dinner on the way home."

She listened a moment in silence.

"Of course I'm safe. I'm with Connor." She smiled over at him.

He smiled back, then frowned again.

"*Bye,* Ethan." She lowered the phone, then pulled it back to her ear. "What? Oh. The Bobcats won, seven-to-five. Thanks for the tickets, by the way."

He said something else. She laughed, then ended the call and stuffed her phone back in her pocket.

"Sounds like Ethan was worried about you."

"He was just being his overprotective self." Annoyance came and went in her eyes. "You'd think I was still seventeen, not six months away from turning thirty."

Connor laughed at her miffed tone. "Don't be too hard on him. It's his job as your big brother to worry about you."

"I never should have told him I was downsized from my last job." She absently shoved at her hair. "He's been overly attentive ever since, like he's waiting for me to fall apart."

Connor didn't get that impression. But before he could say so, she continued.

"I'm not going to fall apart. I have plans. Coming home was the best thing that ever happened to me. I belong here in Village Green."

He liked the sound of that. Maybe too much. "It's good to know where you belong." His reply came out sounding hoarse.

"I should have come home sooner."

"There's no shame in not wanting to leave Florida right away. You'd built a life for yourself there."

"Well, now that I'm here I'm thinking of opening my own tearoom in town, specializing in chocolate desserts."

"You want to start your own business?" Admirable, yet realizing how much time and effort that would take, he felt his stomach rolling. "That's why you left Florida?"

"No, not at first. I left because I... That is, I needed to get away. I couldn't stay any longer because I..."

"Olivia, you don't have to tell me this."

"I know." She held his gaze. "I want to."

"Okay, if you're sure."

She nodded. "I didn't leave because of my job loss or to start my own business in town. Well, not *only* because of those things. I also left because I broke up with my boyfriend."

Connor suddenly felt cold. Ice cold. All this time, he'd assumed Olivia had come into his life with no personal history to speak of and definitely no ex-boyfriends. That had been pretty shortsighted on his part, and maybe even selfish, certainly self-centered, as if his problems were all that mattered.

He looked over at her and his heart took a nose-dive. She was so beautiful. And clearly upset. She'd tugged her bottom lip between her teeth and was twisting her fingers together in her lap.

"Olivia."

Her head turned in his direction. Every single thought flashed in her gaze and Connor realized she regretted sharing her story with him.

That just slayed him.

"About your boyfriend—"

"Warner. His name was, *is* Warner Hartsfield the Fourth."

What a pompous name. Connor disliked the guy already. "Tell me about him," he said through a tight jaw.

"You really want me to?"

He'd rather stick himself in the eye. And that made little sense. It wasn't as if he had any claim on Olivia. She was just his daughters' nanny. "Sure."

"Well...all right." She thought a moment. "He's a successful architect in Jacksonville, one of the best in the state of Florida, actually, and a former All-American quarterback for the University of Miami."

"How did you two meet?"

"At a Super Bowl party." She sighed. "We hit it off right away. He's a single dad and loves his daughter fiercely. His devotion to Kenzie is what I liked most about him."

Connor's throat tightened as he recognized the obvious similarities between him and this Warner dude. "Did his daughter live with him?"

Olivia shook her head. "He shared custody with his ex-wife. I adored her. The daughter, not the ex-wife."

"I figured that."

She gave a humorless laugh. "Warner always said we were a perfect fit. I didn't disagree. We both had successful careers, knew lots of the same people and I got along really well with his daughter. Why not? She's at a really great age."

"How old?"

"Nine. When I lost my job at the bank, Warner pushed for a more serious commitment from me."

Every muscle in Connor's body tensed. "How serious?"

"He asked me to marry him." As still as a rock, she stared up at the sky. Her lovely face stood in profile, projecting an emotion Connor couldn't define. Regret? Disappointment?

"You said no."

"I absolutely said no. Warner didn't love me. I was simply a convenience, especially on visitation weekends. Any number of women could have fit his requirements." She blinked. "He said as much when I told him I didn't want to marry him."

"I'm sorry, Olivia. He didn't deserve you."

"Thank you for that." She drew in a slow, steady breath. "But if I'm being honest with myself, I'd admit that I wasn't much better than Warner. I didn't love him, either. I was only in love with the *idea* of him. He was good-looking, successful and had an adorable daughter whom I cherished."

Connor's chest seized painfully. Did Olivia recognize the similarities between her situation now—with him—and the one she'd just described with her ex-boyfriend? Sure, there were differences. But not many.

"I miss Kenzie." She swiped at her eyes. "But Warner? Not really. What does that say about me?"

"It says that you weren't in love with the guy. You broke things off when you realized that. That doesn't make you a bad person, Olivia. It makes you very wise."

She pressed her fingertips to her temples and rubbed hard. "I'm sorry, Connor. I didn't mean to turn the conversation so heavy. Guess I'm just tired and feeling overly emotional."

"It's been a long day."

"Thank you for listening." She smiled over at him. "Aside from a few speed bumps, it's been a really great day."

Until a few moments ago, Connor would have agreed with her. Now his heart felt unnaturally heavy in his chest. He might have been starting to look at Olivia with more than friendship in mind, but he had to remember she didn't look at him the same way. She had her own hopes and dreams for the future. A tearoom to open. A breakup to get over.

Anything between them just wasn't meant to be.

Chapter Eleven

The next morning, groggy from a restless night's sleep, Olivia woke to the sound of rain slapping against her bedroom window. It was the sort of torrential downpour that didn't show signs of stopping anytime soon. She sighed at the watery world beyond her window. So much for a day at the pool with the girls.

No worries, Olivia would think of an indoor activity for them instead.

Tossing off the bedcovers, she stretched her stiff muscles and thought through her options. A day of baking might be the perfect choice. They hadn't spent much time in the kitchen since she'd taught them how to make frittatas. Why not try out a few new recipes today? She had a great one for chocolate-covered popcorn.

Excited now, she quickly dressed and, deciding not to take Baloo with her for a change, headed across town to Connor's house alone.

Heavy sheets of rain pounded from the sky, making visibility tough. Thunder boomed in the distance. Lightning sizzled and cracked.

Olivia drove with considerable care. She knew this route by heart and the various threats that lurked beneath the car's tires. Still, her hands shook. And her pulse hammered through her veins.

Her parents had died in a storm like this, in early March when the rain had been a vicious mix of sleet and snow. According to the official report, their car had hit a patch of black ice and slid off the road into a ravine.

Willing her mind to release memories of that night, especially when the state trooper had delivered the horrible news, Olivia clutched the steering wheel tighter.

Think about something else, something pleasant.

Her mind immediately went to Connor, the girls and their time together yesterday at the ball field. Every moment had been precious to her. Despite knowing the dangers of getting too close to them, all three Mitchells were becoming a part of her life, a part of her heart.

The realization scared her. And she wondered if she could stop the inevitable from occurring. Or was it too late? Had her life already been changed irrevocably? Was there no going back?

At least she'd told Connor about her breakup with Warner. She hadn't planned on doing that, ever. But she'd been feeling vulnerable after her conversation with the girls about their mother. And Connor had been so understanding, no judgment, no condemnation. His insight had released the guilt she'd been harboring over her role in the breakup.

Yes, she'd fallen into a relationship with a man she hadn't really loved. So she'd stayed with him longer than she should have because of his daughter. At least she'd gotten out before it was too late.

That had to count for something.

Olivia would not allow herself to look back and worry over the mistakes she'd made in the past. It was a new day, a new beginning. Her chance at a new one.

No more planning.

No more putting off finishing her business proposal.

No more waiting for guarantees.

It's go time.

Scary. An uncertain future lay before her, but she had to trust she was on the right track, that the Lord would supply her with the necessary resources and energy.

It all started with faith. Olivia just needed a little more faith.

By the time she arrived at Connor's house, she was ready to begin the rest of her life. Step one, work on several more recipes, with Molly and Megan's help.

The house looked unusually dark, as if the family hadn't risen from their beds yet.

Olivia rushed through the pouring rain and let herself in through the mudroom. She took off her slicker, hung it on a hook and went in search of her family. The kitchen was dark, as well. Odder yet, she encountered no barking, rambunctious puppy spinning out on the tile floor.

"Hello?" Olivia called out, moving through the kitchen into the hallway leading toward the front of the house. "Anyone home?"

She rounded the corner just as Connor exited the girls' bedroom, Samson tucked under his arm. He pulled the door shut and turned to face her. Her breath caught in her throat. He looked...terrible. As if he hadn't slept all night. His hair was a wild mess, his jaw full of stubble, his eyes red-rimmed with fatigue.

"Connor? What's wrong?"

"Molly got sick in the middle of the night." He ran a hand across his mouth. "She woke up just after you left, complaining of a headache and stomachache."

"Too much junk food?"

"I thought so, at first. But then she contracted a fever and a rash broke out on her stomach. Now Megan has a headache, too."

"Chickenpox?"

He nodded.

A thick blanket of tension fell between them. "What can I do to help?"

"For now, nothing. While the girls are asleep I'm going to run out and get some calamine lotion." He shifted the puppy to his other side. "Did you have the virus as a child?"

"I did."

"Good. Then I don't have to worry about you getting sick, too." He wiped at his mouth again, looked around the hallway with half-glazed eyes. "I need to call Ethan, let him know what's going on, that I won't be coming in this morning."

"After you get back from the store, why don't you go crash for a few hours?" She reached for the puppy. "I can take over here."

"I don't think—"

"Connor. I've nursed sick children before. I can handle this. Seriously. Get some rest, Doctor." She laid a hand on his arm, softened her next words with a smile. "That's an order from your nanny."

He stared up at the ceiling, then nodded slowly.

Olivia ran her gaze over his face, wishing she could do more to ease his concerns. He looked wiped out, and really worried about his daughters. Was he remembering his wife's illness? Possibly. He probably thought of it every time one of the twins got sick.

Olivia wanted to weep for him, or maybe pull him into a comforting hug.

She petted the puppy's head instead. "Does he need to go outside?"

"Yeah, but I'll take him before I head to the store."

Nodding, she passed the puppy back.

Connor turned, hesitated. "Thanks, Olivia."

"You're welcome. Now—" she turned him toward the back of the house "—off you go."

As he ambled away, head down, Olivia watched his retreating back with her heart pumping hard. She had to stop herself from chasing after him and giving him that hug, after all.

Oh, Connor. He carried so many burdens, took care of so many people. Who took care of him?

Feeling incredibly helpless, and suddenly in need of a hug herself, Olivia entered the girls' room. She shut the door behind her as quietly as she could.

Molly moaned from her bed and her lashes fluttered open.

"Hi there, sweetie," Olivia said softly, hoping not to avoid waking Megan, who tossed and turned fitfully in her sleep. "I hear you're not feeling so well."

"My head hurts. I ache everywhere." She kicked her legs out from under the covers. "And I'm hot. Really hot."

Olivia sat on the bed, swept Molly's hair off her forehead and felt the urge to weep again. The poor thing looked miserable.

This particular Mitchell she did pull into a comforting hug. "It's going to be okay, sweetie."

"Promise?"

"Promise."

Unsure how long he'd slept, Connor checked the time on his phone. Just shy of 11:00 a.m. He'd been out nearly three hours. Way too long.

He jumped out of bed, rubbed an impatient hand down his face, glanced around until he had his bearings. He needed to check on the girls, shower and shave, then hopefully get to the office before noon. It was a good plan, as long as the girls weren't any worse. Everything depended on their condition.

He exited his bedroom.

Normally, he wouldn't consider leaving the girls while they were sick. But Olivia was here. He trusted her with them completely and was coming to rely on her, perhaps more than he should.

Was he expecting too much from a temporary nanny, unconsciously taking Olivia for granted, as that Warner character had done?

Connor would be reckless to forget the story she'd told him about her ex-boyfriend. Unwise and thoughtless to think she wasn't still wounded from the experience. He'd seen the tears in her eyes last night, the ones she'd tried to hide from him.

Olivia stepped out of the girls' room just as Connor rounded the corner. She looked tired, a bit disheveled, yet incredibly beautiful.

Spotting him, she smiled. Her big blue eyes were filled with sympathy for his daughters. His heart swelled.

"How are they?"

"Uncomfortable, hurting. Starting to itch. And really, really bored, especially Molly." She made a vague gesture with her hand toward the bedroom behind her. "I'm going to hunt down some coloring books, crayons and puzzles. Maybe that'll entertain both girls while I try to think up some other non-physical activities besides television to keep them occupied."

"Good idea. You'll find what you're looking for in the living room, third shelf on the right-hand side of the bookcase."

"I remember." She turned to go, then spun back around and considered him a moment in silence. "You look better than you did this morning, more rested."

"I am." And he owed it to Olivia. For that single reason, he took a step back, physically and emotionally.

"You push yourself too hard, Connor. I'm glad you took a much-needed break."

He felt his heart catch hard at her words, at the smile she gave him, and all he could do was manage a quick "Thanks, Olivia," before he stepped into the girls' room and shut himself inside.

Goofy cartoon music swelled from the television on the dresser. Samson lay silently on Megan's feet, blinking up at Connor as if afraid to move. Neither of his daughters were paying attention to the screen, so he reached over and turned off the program.

"Hey." Arms crossed over her chest, chin jutting out, Molly looked disgruntled by the move. "I was watching that."

"No, you weren't."

She pressed her lips into a small, thin line. "I was getting ready to."

He ignored this, took in her angry eyes and heightened color. "How are you feeling?"

Grimacing, Molly gave him a world-weary sigh. Quite a feat for an eight-year-old. "I'm bored."

"Miss Olivia will be back with some coloring books and crayons."

"Coloring is for babies."

Connor chose not to comment, especially since Molly had colored a picture for him just two days ago. The one that still hung on the refrigerator door, front and center.

"How about you, Megan?" He turned his focus on his other daughter. "How are you feeling?"

"Really itchy, but Miss Olivia says I can't scratch."

"Miss Olivia is right."

"My head hurts, too."

"I'm sorry about that." Connor sat on Megan's bed, smoothed her hair off her red face. "You probably need some more medicine. But first, let me see your neck."

She obediently lifted her chin.

He probed beneath her jawline. Definitely swollen lymph nodes, but no more than expected given the circumstances. Her skin was unnaturally hot to the touch, though. A quick stab of panic shot through him, but he reminded himself this was the twenty-first century. Children didn't die of chickenpox. Especially healthy, robust children like his daughters. No reason to be alarmed.

Forcing out a slow breath, he checked Megan's temperature with the digital thermometer—101.2.

He switched beds and checked Molly's—101.1.

Higher than he'd prefer, but not totally unexpected.

He took the water bottle off Megan's nightstand and handed it over. "Drink some of this."

"What about me?" Molly whined, tears of frustration brimming in her eyes. "Don't I get some water, too?"

"Coming right up." He located her bottle, unscrewed the cap and passed it to her.

She took a long, gulping drink.

"Better?"

She took another, smaller sip. "Much."

"Look what I found." Arms full, Olivia reentered the room. "Coloring books, puzzles, word searches and crayons. A whole assortment of things for us to do today."

She dumped the entire load on Molly's bed, reached over and scratched Samson behind the ears.

Molly feigned total disinterest in the booty at her feet, until her sister asked to see the coloring book with the princesses on the front. Molly decided that was the one item she wanted most.

Just as an argument ensued, Olivia stepped in a second before Connor could. "There's actually two with princesses on them." She retrieved both. "One for each of you."

Connor watched, marveling, as Olivia set up his daughters with their own lap desk, coloring book and box of crayons.

Disaster avoided.

"Okay." She brushed off her hands. "I'm going to have a quick word with your father and then I'll be back to color with you."

Before any of them could object, including Connor, Olivia tugged him out of the room. "I thought the girls might also like to embellish some T-shirts while they're stuck in their beds."

Connor suppressed a sigh. Sounded a little too girly for him. But Olivia was probably right. She knew more about these things than he did. "What would that involve?"

"A trip to the craft store." She dug a piece of paper out of her back pocket. "Would you mind going?"

He chuckled. "If I didn't know better I'd say you were trying to get rid of me."

She didn't deny it. "I figure one of us has to stay with the twins, might as well be me. I can make us all lunch while you're gone."

His stomach growled, reminding him that he'd missed breakfast.

"I'm making chicken soup for the girls and I was thinking grilled cheese sandwiches for us."

"My favorite."

"I know."

How'd she know that?

Seizing his moment of hesitation, she pressed the piece of paper in his hand. "We'll need everything on the list. The salesgirl will help you if you get lost."

Connor laughed. She managed to get him to do what she wanted without sounding bossy. "I bet you were a killer in the boardroom."

"I do know how to get my way." She wiggled her eyebrows at him. "Especially when it's something as important as rhinestones and T-shirts for sick little girls."

Connor could fall hard for this woman, if he let himself.

Fortunately, he understood Olivia better than he had that first day in the park, especially after their conversation last night. Her unexpected job loss hadn't been her only reason for coming home. A broken relationship had also led her back to Village Green.

Despite the decision being hers, she was still hurting, still vulnerable. Still working through what she wanted to do with her life.

Connor would be wise to keep his distance.

He'd better keep his distance.

How was he going to keep his distance?

Chapter Twelve

Three days after the twins' fever finally broke, and their itching was under control, Connor insisted Olivia take the weekend off. She'd protested, telling him she only needed one free day a week, but he'd refused to budge.

Out of arguments, she'd accepted his kind offer, spending most of Saturday working on her business proposal. Thanks to the uninterrupted time, she was nearly done with it.

She woke early Sunday morning with plans to attend services with Keely at the church they'd attended as teenagers. According to her friend, one of her brother Beau's buddies had gone to seminary in Louisville, Kentucky, and was now the senior pastor.

Keely said he gave a great sermon.

Olivia couldn't wait to hear for herself. She'd been away from church too long. Ever since she'd broken up with Warner and moved home.

She quickly dressed and caught up with Ethan in

the kitchen. He wore jeans and a ratty T-shirt as old as Olivia and was downing a large mug of coffee in big, manly gulps.

"Hope you left some for me."

Smiling, he stepped around Baloo, whose tail whipped around like a deadly weapon, and poured Olivia a cup.

With the easygoing, affectionate older brother in place, he handed over the coffee. "Got any plans for the day?"

"Church." Then she would put the finishing touches on her business proposal this afternoon. Once that was done to her satisfaction, she could set up an appointment at the bank and start the process of securing a loan. *Make a plan. Work the plan. Adjust when necessary.*

No more dragging her feet. The summer would be over soon.

"Right, it's Sunday. I tend to forget what day it is when I'm not working." He turned his back on her, the move sufficiently cutting off whatever reply she would have given him.

While he rinsed his cup in the sink, she shifted from one foot to the other, opened her mouth to speak, but then her phone buzzed a warning that a text message had just come through. She looked down and read the screen. It was from Keely. SERVICE STARTS IN TWENTY MINUTES. "Gotta go."

"Go?" Ethan spun around. "Where?"

"To church, remember?" She typed a quick response. ON MY WAY. Then stuffed the phone back in her purse. "Want to come with me?"

"No."

"I'm meeting my friend Keely," she said. "We're sitting together."

"Then definitely no."

How odd. Olivia angled her head. "You have something against Keely?"

"Nope. Not a thing." He turned his back on her again, pulled Baloo's leash off the wall hook and clipped it in the dog's collar. "Come on, boy, let's go for a walk."

Baloo's tail slapped like a whip as Ethan guided him to the back door. Man and dog were gone before Olivia could take another sip of her coffee.

"Well, that was…interesting."

Shrugging, she fished her keys out of her purse and left through the front door. The church was only a block north of her brother's medical offices, easy walking distance from the house, but the weather didn't look promising enough to risk the short trek on foot.

Five minutes later, Olivia pulled into the parking lot, hoping she'd run into the Mitchell family today. She hadn't seen the girls since Friday.

She missed them like crazy, worried about them, hoped they were feeling back to normal.

Connor had answered her text yesterday and said the girls were on the mend. And that he would see her on Monday morning, same time as always.

The man was back to being distant with her again. That was probably for the best. Nevertheless, a slow sigh slipped past her lips.

The church's parking lot was just short of chaotic. Olivia managed to find a free spot in the middle row. Hurrying out of her car, she rushed over to where Keely waited for her on the church steps. Connor's sister, Avery, stood beside the redhead. The twins were next to their aunt. But there was no sign of Connor.

Where was he?

Olivia looked around, checking several groups.

"Miss Olivia, Miss Olivia," Molly called out, waving her hands frantically in the air. "Over here. We're over here."

Megan spun around and squealed when she saw Olivia approaching.

Olivia's sentiments exactly.

Attacking the steps two at a time, she closed the distance between them at a near run, then tugged both girls into her arms. She knew she'd lost objectivity. And had completely forgotten to guard her heart.

At the moment, Olivia didn't much care. How would life ever be worth living if she went through it guarding her heart against love?

Over their heads she greeted Keely and Avery, then put all her attention on the twins. "How are you feeling?"

"So much better."

And so began a fast-paced litany of all the things they wanted to do now that they were back to normal. "A slumber party would be pretty awesome," Molly decided. "With just us girls, no boys allowed."

"Then let's have a slumber party very soon," Olivia said.

"We can have it at my house," Avery offered. "As long as your dad says it's okay."

"My dad's cool with it," Keely offered up, grinning.

"Ha-ha." Avery flicked her wrist at the redhead. "I was talking about Connor."

"Speaking of Connor." Olivia looked around, scanned the immediate area. "Where is he?"

Megan touched her hand. "Daddy went into the office to catch up on email."

"He always goes into the office on Sunday mornings," Molly added.

Seconds ticked by before that piece of information sank in. "Oh."

The praise band started warming up, the sound drifting through the front doors and alerting everyone that church would begin soon.

"Hey, Olivia, save me a seat next to you and Keely." Avery hooked an arm over Megan's shoulders, then Molly's. "I have to take these munchkins over to children's church. I'll meet you in the worship center when I'm done."

"You got it."

Keely waited until they were both settled in chairs

along the back row, before leaning toward Olivia and whispering, "I was so excited to see you last week I totally forgot to ask if you'd like to join our women's Bible study. We meet every Friday morning around sevenish at the Turkey Roost."

"Sounds awesome," Olivia said.

"We call ourselves the BBS girls."

Her eyes narrowed. "BBS?"

"Breakfast and Bible Study. BBS, get it?"

Olivia laughed. "Count me in."

"Count you in where?" Avery asked from the aisle, her eyebrows lifted in question.

Keely grinned up at her. "I was just telling Olivia about our Friday morning Bible study. She's going to join us."

"Awesome."

With her purse the size of a small rhino slung over her shoulder, Avery sidled in next to Olivia.

The opening song began a second later.

The entire congregation rose to their feet, the three women included.

Olivia did her best to focus on worship. She managed to do so on the first two songs. By the third she couldn't hold back her curiosity any longer.

"Connor goes into work every Sunday morning instead of attending church?" she whispered to Avery.

The other woman sighed heavily. "He drops off the girls but never sticks around. And I mean never."

"How long has this been going on?"

Avery sighed again. "Since Sheila's funeral."

Oh, Connor.

Connor arrived back at the church a few minutes before the service let out. He'd attempted to get some work done in the office but hadn't been able to make his brain focus longer than a few minutes at a time. He eventually gave up and let his mind wander. Which it did.

Straight to Olivia.

He'd seen the way his daughters had soared into her arms. The three of them had looked thrilled over their reunion, as if they'd been apart for years rather than a few days. Linked together in a single embrace, practically clinging to one another, they'd looked like a family.

Family. Something he just might be ready to expand beyond him and the twins. And he wasn't thinking in terms of adding another dog.

There was a shift occurring in him, in his body and soul, a sort of letting go of the old and grasping for the new. As if he were waking from a long, fitful sleep.

He sank down on the church steps, placed his elbows on his knees and absently watched the Sunday-morning traffic meander past.

In that moment, he felt like a fraud. Family. Future. He had no business asking any woman to share either of them with him until he let go of his anger.

Toward God. Toward himself. Both were intricately linked, neither existing without the other.

He knew he had to make peace with the past, with himself and with God, before he could claim the peace *of* God.

Where did he begin?

His anger ran deep. Sheila had died too soon after they'd put their marriage back together. They'd only had a few months of genuine harmony before everything had fallen apart again.

He gives and He takes away.

Why, Lord?

Connor had followed the rules. He'd put family ahead of work and his marriage ahead of ambition. He'd chosen general practice over a more demanding specialty. And still, the Lord sentenced two little girls to go through life without their mother.

Molly and Megan were hungry for female attention, as evidenced by their quick attachment to Olivia. Not that Connor didn't understand their fascination with the woman. He was becoming attached to Olivia himself.

But he couldn't forget that she had plans to start her own business. Connor knew what demands she would face on her time, on her heart, the kind that had nearly ruined his marriage to Sheila. There wouldn't be room in Olivia's life for much other than work, at least in the early years.

The sound of a familiar praise song wafted on the

air. Connor's eyes burned as the words drifted over him. "I will rise up like wings on eagles."

He squeezed his eyes shut, willing the image of his wife to come to him. Instead of Sheila's blond hair and lean, athletic build, the image that filled his mind was of a woman with dark hair, blue, blue eyes and a smile that nearly knocked him off his feet.

Another shift occurred inside him, away from things he'd always known, toward unchartered territory.

He thought he might be sick.

The doors swung open behind him and out came the first wave of people.

Connor stood aside to let them pass. His gaze found Olivia the moment she exited the church. He tried to gather the wits necessary to look away.

He couldn't.

People continued spilling out of the church. Some rushed past him. Others smiled or called a greeting, acknowledging him with a wave or head bob from wherever they stood.

His throat clogged at the unrestrained acceptance they displayed toward him. No pressure. No comments about his absence over the years. Just smiles and a few kind words.

And there was Olivia, watching him with a look in her eyes similar to all the others, yet with a slightly different spin, a more personal one.

The choke hold around his heart released and everything in him simply…let…go.

For a brief moment, Connor couldn't move, couldn't breathe, couldn't break eye contact.

Olivia appeared equally frozen in place.

Another moment of staring passed, and then Avery came into view, moving between them with a smirk on her face. She made a grand show of looking from one to the other, then strolled over to him. "Hey. You okay?"

"Sure." But his throat burned. And his heart ached.

Swallowing hard, he concentrated on his sister's face.

Bad idea. Avery was smirking at him, with a knowing twinkle in her eyes. "You look like someone smacked you upside the head."

Sometimes little sisters were nothing but an annoyance. "It's been a long day."

"Uh-huh." She slanted a look at Olivia.

Connor followed the direction of her gaze. Another bad idea. The very worst of bad ideas.

Olivia was now engaged in a conversation with Keely O'Toole's hotshot brother, a man who seemed to be standing entirely too close, with entirely too much interest in his eyes.

Beau said something that made Olivia playfully slap at his arm. Connor's knee-jerk response was to start up the steps in their direction.

Avery stopped him with a laugh. "In my professional medical opinion—"

"You aren't a doctor yet."

"I will be soon." She ratcheted up the annoying little-sister grin. "Besides, it doesn't take a medical degree to know the signs of a man in—"

"Where are the twins?"

"Still in children's church, as you well know. And, wow, Connor." Eyes luminous with sympathy, she squeezed his arm. "You really got it bad for the nanny."

He ignored the comment, though he privately agreed with his sister. He wanted nothing more than to take Olivia in his arms and unleash a load of promises he wasn't sure he could keep. Or worse, she wouldn't want him to give.

He'd be wise to keep his distance. With that in mind, he started off in the direction of the children's building.

"Before you go." Avery's voice stopped him in his tracks. "I invited Olivia and her friend Keely to Sunday dinner at your house this afternoon. Hope that was all right."

Since Connor had begun hosting Sunday dinner, he'd insisted the table include more than immediate family. Friends, neighbors, people in need. The different mix always made for an interesting afternoon. "Of course."

"So you're okay that I invited them?"

"You know I am," he said, wondering why she felt the need to ask a second time. "You can invite anyone you want."

"Oh, good." She clapped her hands together in

delight. "Then I'm going to invite Keely's brother, too. That okay with you?"

Despite not liking the way the guy eyed Olivia, there was no real reason to say no.

"Fine. Invite him." He spoke flatly, with only a hint of sarcasm in his tone. "The more the merrier."

"Try to drum up some enthusiasm."

He bared his teeth. "That better?"

"Perfect." Laughing, she proceeded to saunter over to Beau O'Toole.

One good thing about Avery asking the guy to Sunday dinner. Beau was forced to turn away from Olivia to give his answer.

Chapter Thirteen

Sunday dinner at Connor's house proved to be a lot of fun. Chaotic, yes. But that was what made the day special. Besides, Olivia decided, a certain level of mayhem was to be expected with the broad mix of adults, children, dogs and one rambunctious puppy.

Ethan and Ryder had even shown up with Baloo. They'd arrived just as Olivia, Keely and Avery had begun serving the meal.

Her brothers had uncanny timing when it came to home-cooked meals. They always managed to appear at the precise moment the food hit the table.

Olivia shook her head, filled a second bowl of mashed potatoes and headed outside to deliver it to the long picnic table Connor had set up for the occasion.

Despite the sketchy weather earlier this morning, the sun shone brightly now, a big, fat yellow ball against a clear blue sky.

Connor met her halfway across the yard and took

the bowl from her. Their fingers touched, just a gentle slide of his over hers, and yet all five of her senses went on high alert.

How'd he do that?

No man had ever pulled this reaction out of her, simply because of a barely-there touch. Not Warner, not her college boyfriend, not even Keely's brother, Beau. Who was arguably one of the most charming, best-looking men in town. Besides Connor.

Laid-back, easygoing, Beau O'Toole was the quintessential poster boy for Colorado ski country. The startling green eyes and messy, sun-kissed brown hair added to his overall appeal.

But Olivia had known him all her life and knew he went through women like a camel went through water after a trip across the desert. Beau might seem interested in her, today, and had already asked her out three times since the church service let out, but Olivia knew better. He was just being Beau.

Even if he'd been sincere, she'd never go out with him. For the simple reason he wasn't Connor.

Why him? Why now, when Olivia had plans that required her full concentration? If all went according to the timetable she'd recently devised, she would be securing a loan in the coming weeks.

So, again, why Connor? Why now?

She knew the answer, of course. Because, as her mother used to say, the heart wants what the heart wants.

"Get yourself a plate of food," he said, still standing with the bowl between them. "You're looking a little pale."

Hunger had nothing to do with her condition. A hope for something that might never be hers, hope for a family that needed her desperately, perhaps for all the wrong reasons. Those things, added together, could definitely cause a loss of color.

"Go on." He nudged her with his shoulder.

She remained firmly in place. "Have *you* eaten?"

"I will, once everyone else has been served."

His answer was a telling one. Connor was always taking care of everyone, putting himself last. The dedicated father, the caring big brother, the overworked doctor.

Who took care of Connor?

"Let's eat together," she suggested, taking the potatoes back. "After I deliver these to the table."

He simply stared at her.

"We'll both get a plate and sit over there—" she hitched her chin to her left "—under the tree by the pond."

He continued staring at her. And for the first time since knowing him, Connor Mitchell looked as if he were unable to make a decision.

He quickly recovered. "Excellent suggestion. I'd like to talk to you about something anyway."

Looking as if he had more to say, he was interrupted when Ethan's voice lifted over the crowd. "One of you gonna serve those potatoes before they get cold?"

Olivia hurried away.

The rest of the afternoon went by in a haze. She never did get a chance to sit down and eat with Connor. Or anyone, for that matter. She'd picked her way through a meal while making sure everyone else was served.

She still had a great day.

About an hour before dusk, after a fourth game of volleyball, people started leaving. By the time the sun drew even with the horizon, there were only a few stragglers. Beau left right after Ethan, Baloo and Ryder. Keely hadn't been far behind since she had to cover the dinner shift at her restaurant.

When the girls started bickering over who lost Samson's ball in the pond—a sure sign of their mutual exhaustion—Olivia ushered them inside the house. She set them up with a movie and one very tuckered out puppy settled on the sofa between them.

The three fell asleep before Olivia pressed Play on the remote in her hand.

Padding quietly back through the house, she found Avery in the kitchen, filling the sink with soapy water. "I can do that," she said.

"I'm good." She smiled over her shoulder. "But I wouldn't turn away help."

"You got it." Olivia grabbed a towel and began drying the dishes Avery had already washed.

They stood side by side, working in silence, their gazes focused on the window that overlooked the backyard.

Connor was out there alone, clearing away trash, breaking down tables and chairs, looking like the man in charge, as if the world stood on his shoulders and he was managing just fine. Thank you, very much.

"Does he ever relax?" she wondered aloud.

"Not nearly enough." Avery sounded every bit as worried as Olivia felt. "Since Sheila died he's worked three times as hard to create a happy life for the girls. Though he'd never admit it, the brutal schedule he's set for himself is taking a toll. I can see it in the lines around his eyes and mouth."

Olivia thought about the twins, how well-adjusted they were, especially considering they barely remembered their mother. Connor had kept her alive in their hearts with pictures and stories, and his daughters had reaped the benefits. "He's a good man."

"The very best," Avery agreed. "And the most stubborn one on the planet."

Olivia knew at least three others that could compete for the title, all with the last name Scott. But none of her brothers were single fathers, so maybe Connor was the most stubborn of them all. Certainly the hardest-working of the bunch. "I wish he would, I don't know..." She picked up another plate and wiped the water away. "I wish he'd let someone help him out."

Avery looked over at her. "He has help. Carlotta is a wonder. And you've managed to provide in her absence."

Then why did Olivia feel as if she were failing him? "That's not what I meant."

"What did you mean?"

Eyes still on Connor, she thought about the night the girls came down with the chickenpox and how much he sacrificed for them on a daily basis. Who made sacrifices on his behalf?

"He doesn't just need someone to help him around the house. He needs someone…to…" She swallowed hard. "Love him."

"From where I'm standing—" Avery turned off the faucet and took the towel from Olivia to dry her hands "—I'd say someone already does. And I'm not talking about immediate family members."

Olivia simply sighed.

Avery passed her back the towel. "Can I give you a piece of advice?"

"Um…okay."

"Don't give up on my brother."

Olivia's throat seized, and she had to blink several times to keep her eyes dry. "You're making assumptions about our relationship. I'm just the nanny, only here temporarily until Carlotta's knee heals."

"We both know you're more than that."

Was she? Olivia felt a rush of hope surge through her blood.

"For all his competence in the medical field, and in so many other areas of his life, Connor's never had to pursue a woman." She pulled Olivia to an empty chair and pressed on her shoulders until she sat. "He's going to stumble around at first, maybe even push you away if things get too heavy."

Eaten alive with hope, yet afraid to let herself give in to the emotion, Olivia stared into Avery's eyes. "What if he's not interested in me that way?"

"Oh, he's interested."

"You seem awfully sure of that."

"That's because I am." Avery grinned. "Whenever you enter a room, his eyes track straight to you. You're the only woman I've ever seen him look at like that. It's kind of sweet and icky at the same time."

Olivia laughed.

Avery joined in. "And if that wasn't enough of a giveaway, he really didn't like seeing you flirting with Beau today."

"I wasn't flirting with Beau."

Avery gave her a get-real roll of her eyes.

"*He* was flirting with *me*."

"Okay, fair enough. The point is that Connor wasn't happy watching you two together."

Even if he was interested in her, would he be able to let Sheila go? Enough to love another woman? To love Olivia?

She didn't know. The not knowing scared her, because she thought she might be falling for him. Despite her efforts to guard her heart, to remember what it was like to be nothing more than a convenience in a man's life, Connor and his daughters had slipped through her defenses.

"You're going to have to stand firm, Olivia, and maybe do a bit of the pursuing yourself if Connor drags his feet."

"Why are you telling me this, Avery?"

"Because I like you, always have."

Olivia smiled. "I like you, too."

"Glad we're in full agreement." She sat next to Olivia in the empty chair beside her. "You're good for my brother, and that's not something I take lightly. You shouldn't, either."

As she mulled this over, Olivia realized something else. Not only was she good for Connor; he was good for her. They might even be better together than apart.

One problem. "What if he doesn't let me in?"

"Then you push your way in."

That would require some serious nerve. And a lot of hard work on her part. She'd have to make herself vulnerable again, to risk terrible hurt, perhaps worse than the one she'd recently suffered.

Did Olivia have the courage? The fortitude? Of course she did. She was a Scott. Scotts never gave up. They never backed down. They went after what they wanted.

Nevertheless, pushing her way into Connor's heart wouldn't be easy. There would probably be times when Olivia would wonder what she'd gotten herself into. But one thing she knew for sure. Connor Mitchell and his two daughters were keepers, and totally worth the effort.

* * *

Connor entered the kitchen moments after the su
disappeared behind the mountains, leaving the sk
a soft gray awash with fading pinks, oranges an
purples. Avery and Olivia were in deep conversa
tion, their heads bent closely together, probably dis
cussing things no man should overhear.

Seeking quick escape, he carefully backtracke
in the direction he came. One step. Two.

Avery lifted her head. "Ah, Connor. There yo
are. Olivia and I were just finishing up."

"Looks like you were just getting started."

"Nope, we're all through." Avery hopped to he
feet.

At the same moment, Olivia glanced at him ove
her shoulder. There was something new in her eyes
something determined and very female. Connor sud
denly felt like a prize buck caught in the crosshair
of a wily hunter.

It wasn't a thoroughly awful sensation.

"I think I hear the girls calling me." Avery prac
tically ran out of the room. But then she stoppe
and turned back to Olivia. "Want me to set up ou
slumber party for next weekend?"

Her eyes still locked and loaded on Connor, Olivi
nodded. "I'd love that. Thanks for suggesting it."

"It'll be fun." Avery sauntered out, leaving Con
nor alone with Olivia.

"Grown women still have slumber parties?"

"Sure they do. Avery's planning a girls' night a

her house, or rather your parents' house now that she's staying there over the summer." She rose from her chair and stepped toward him. "There'll be chick flicks, junk food, hair braiding, fingernail painting. The works."

He couldn't help himself. He shuddered.

Smiling now, Olivia drew closer. "The twins are invited to come along."

"No kidding?"

"They're girls, aren't they?"

"Last I heard."

"Then they're invited to join us. We might even talk about—" she lowered her voice to a whisper "—*boys*. It'll be fun for them. I'll make sure we keep the conversation age-appropriate. You can approve the movies we pick, and—"

"Olivia, you don't have to sell me on the idea. I'm on board." He touched her shoulder. "I trust you with my daughters."

He moved his hand down her arm, stopped when his fingers linked with hers. Everything in him softened, settled. Standing like this, holding hands with Olivia, smiling at her, it felt as natural as breathing.

And just as fundamental.

Highly unexpected, and equally profound.

"Olivia." He spoke her name on an exhale, the word barely audible. "In all the chaos of the last week, I never thanked you for taking care of the girls when they were sick."

Her eyes fluttered. "I was just doing my job."

They both knew her devotion and attentiveness to their needs had been more than that. She'd cared for the twins as if they'd been her own daughters. "Still, thank you. I don't how I would have managed without you."

She flinched, the long, quiet stare she gave him accomplishing more than words. She'd misunderstood his meaning. "I don't take anything you do in my home for granted." He tucked a strand of hair behind her ear. "I don't take *you* for granted. promise I never will."

"Oh, Connor."

She managed to convey a world of emotion in those two words, a depth of feeling that matched the changes growing inside him, changes that had begun that first day in Hawkins Park.

Something ignited in his heart, something he'd thought long dead, a feeling dangerously close to hope. Hope for the future.

With a woman other than Sheila.

Not nearly as shocked by the revelation as he should be, he smiled down at Olivia.

She said nothing. Apparently, he'd left her speechless. He wasn't feeling wordy himself. He was, however, feeling young, free. *Alive.*

Samson whizzed into the kitchen, heading for.. who knew where? The dumb animal overshot his mark and began backpedaling. Too late. He'd already lost control. He skidded into the leg of the kitchen table. And bounced.

Equilibrium regained, he spun around and hurried over to Olivia. All politeness now, he plopped his bottom on the floor and gazed up at her.

The look of adoration on the mutt's face probably mirrored Connor's own expression. There were only two males in the Mitchell household, and they were both big, dopey saps.

Olivia had that way about her.

And Connor had a lot of thinking to do.

Several obstacles stood between him and Olivia, mostly on her end. Some on his. He had to think about his daughters most of all, and what a relationship with Olivia would mean to them. Especially if it failed.

"I bet you think it's dinnertime," Olivia said to the poor besotted animal blinking up at her with adoring eyes.

A single bark was Samson's heartfelt response.

Olivia showed him her palm. "Stay."

Shockingly, Samson stayed while she filled his bowl from the bag of kibble in the pantry.

"Someone's been training our dog," Connor said, marveling as she set the bowl on the floor and Samson calmly dug into his dinner.

"Miss Olivia's been training him," Molly announced as she and Megan entered the kitchen with Avery tagging along. The smug expression on his sister's face told Connor she had a good idea what had happened in her absence.

Connor tried not to sigh.

"Samson only listens sometimes," Megan informed him. "But he's a good boy. You're a good boy, aren't you, Samson?"

The dog lifted his head briefly, then proceeded to devour the rest of his dinner. No chewing, but a lot of swallowing.

Giggling, Megan reached down and scratched behind the dog's ears in a gesture that reminded Connor of Olivia.

The woman was making an impression on them all. Connor needed to take a step back, literally and figuratively. He needed to think, measure, evaluate.

What would happen when Carlotta returned and Olivia was no longer in his home? What would happen when she put her full focus on opening her own business? Her free time would be virtually nonexistent. It would be hard enough for Connor. No telling how the twins would take the loss of seeing her every day. They'd become pretty attached. Okay, really attached. A problem he hadn't thought through when he'd hired Olivia.

But a consideration he must contemplate now.

One thing at a time, he reminded himself, and decided to come up with a workable exit strategy later. For now, he settled on enjoying the rest of the evening with his girls. All three of them.

Plus one smirking younger sister with a knowing gleam in her eyes.

Chapter Fourteen

Olivia turned her key in the ignition, heard a click, click, click, then…nothing.

Watching from outside the driver's-side window, Avery leaned her head in the car. "Connor says try it again."

Pressing her lips in a grim line, Olivia rotated the key yet again. Click, click, click. Then, like every other time…*nothing*.

A sigh leaked past her tight lips.

Why wasn't her car starting? She'd watched Connor clip the jumper cables to her battery and the other end to the one in his SUV.

The sound of tinkering and muttering came from the other side of her popped hood, and then Connor joined Avery outside Olivia's window. "It's not the battery."

Of course it was the battery. "Are you sure your jumper cables are working?"

"It's not the battery," he repeated.

She frowned. "But the red indicator light is flashing." She jabbed her finger toward the dashboard. "See for yourself."

He peered into the car and studied the light with a serious expression. "Then it's the starter."

"Oh." That sounded simple enough. "Can you fix it?"

The question earned her a low chuckle. "I'm not a mechanic, Olivia. You're going to have to call a garage to pick up your car."

"But…" She shoved a clump of hair away from her eyes. "It's Sunday evening. No garage is open at this hour."

"You'll have to leave your car here overnight and we'll call the garage to come tow it away in the morning."

What a hassle.

"Sounds like a workable plan to me. Now stop scowling, both of you." Sounding utterly unconcerned by Olivia's predicament, Avery pulled her from the car and steered her over to the SUV. "In the meantime, Connor can give you a ride home."

"Why can't you do it?" she asked her friend.

Trying unsuccessfully to hold back a smile, Avery slanted Olivia an *oh, please* look. "Because I want to spend quality time with my nieces, that's why. And besides, Connor's car is right here." Avery nudged Olivia a few more steps. "And mine is halfway down the gravel road."

Eyebrows raised, Connor remained silent during

Avery's unnecessarily long explanation. But he didn't balk over her suggestion. Instead, he said, "Hang tight, Olivia." He took the jumper cables off each battery, stowed them in the back of his SUV and then shut both hoods. "Let me tell the girls where I'm going and we'll head out."

The moment he disappeared in the house, Avery let out a slow whoosh of air. "I am so good." She slid her arm through Olivia's and grinned. "Notice how my brother jumped on my suggestion to give you a lift home."

Actually, Olivia hadn't noticed. And now that Avery had pointed it out, she told herself not to read too much into it. Connor was a gentleman to the core. Hesitating to give her a ride home would have gone against his character.

By the time he returned, Olivia had already retrieved her keys and purse from her car.

After telling Olivia goodbye, Avery hustled back toward the house with a promise to see Connor when he got back.

His unreadable expression didn't change once she disappeared in the house. Ever the gentleman, he opened the passenger door for Olivia and waited until she clicked on her seat belt before coming around to his side of the car to do the same.

Despite Connor's silence as he navigated out the drive and onto Aspen Way, Olivia relaxed back in her seat and closed her eyes.

"Tired?" The question washed over her in a smooth, easy baritone, relaxing her further.

"A little." She opened her eyes and swiveled her head to look at him. "You know, Connor, hosting Sunday dinner at your house every week, it's a really great thing to do. Everyone had a good time."

"Did you?"

"Yes." She let out a quick laugh. "I really, really did. I can see why you want to keep the tradition going now that your parents have left town."

His smile came and went so fast she nearly missed it. "Thanks for helping Avery out with all the cooking. You didn't have to do that."

"I wanted to."

"Still…" He braked for a red light, then turned to look at her. "That's not why you were invited. You were supposed to be a guest today. I don't want you to think every time I host a function at my house, you have to work in the kitchen."

His sincerity, as much as the words themselves, sent her blood hammering through her veins. She felt hot, then cold, then warm all over as his earlier comment came back to her. *I don't take you for granted. I promise I never will.* Did he know how much those words meant to her?

How they made her fall a little in love with him, even though she'd attempted to guard her heart?

"Oh, Connor. I really didn't mind cooking today. I actually had fun. It gave me a chance to try out a few more recipes, including my newest one for potato salad."

The light changed and he pressed on the gas. "Recipes? You mean for your restaurant?"

"For my tearoom," she corrected. "And, yes, I'm building a menu as part of my business plan. Best way to know what to include is to test out various dishes on as many people as I can."

"That makes sense."

He seemed captured by the road up ahead, freeing her to study him without interruption. He had a great profile, strong jawline, nicely proportioned nose, well-arched eyebrows that were pulled together in concentration. "Sounds like you've really thought this venture through and your plans are progressing."

"I'm determined to make a go of this. If not now, when?"

He nodded. But she noticed his hands tightened on the steering wheel, wondered at it. "Have you been trying out recipes on the girls and me?"

"Absolutely. That's okay, isn't it?"

"It's more than okay." He stopped at another light, appeared to debate something with himself, then turned to face her. "If you'd told me sooner I could have offered my own expertise."

"In the kitchen?"

He laughed. "No way. But I know people at several banks in town and a few in Denver. You probably don't need any help with a business plan, but

I can certainly introduce you to loan officers, including Hardy Bennett. He gave me my first loan."

She blinked at him. "You'd do that for me?"

"It'd be my pleasure, especially since I'm no help in the kitchen."

"The girls have been helping me there. They really enjoy working with chocolate."

That teased out a wisp of a smile from him. "They are my daughters."

"They're great girls, Connor. It's been a joy watching them this summer." *I wish they were mine.* "You've done an excellent job raising them."

His smile disappeared. "I can't help thinking I could do more."

"You do enough already."

He shook his head. "Not nearly. The girls will be entering a new stage in their lives very soon. They're going to need a woman in their lives who can help them navigate the dangerous waters of adolescence."

The burst of longing to be that woman came fast and hard, shocking Olivia with its intensity. Scaring her a little.

A sigh slipped out of her. "They have Avery and your other sisters."

"That's true. But Avery is leaving for medical school and the other three don't live in Village Green anymore. Even if they did, that's not what I had in mind. Molly and Megan need a mother."

Olivia's heart went *zing*.

There he was, Connor Mitchell, handsome and

very male, speaking the truth from his heart, and sounding a little too much like Warner for comfort.

Olivia swallowed back a sudden wave of disappointment and maybe a little fear. Had she just landed herself in a scenario similar to the one she'd left back in Florida?

Could she be that reckless?

As if reading her mind, Connor pulled the car to a stop outside her house, cut the engine and shifted in his seat. "But as much as the girls need a mother, I'd never marry a woman for that reason alone. That wouldn't be fair to any of us."

Relief would have buckled her knees had she been standing. "You're absolutely right."

"You understand what I'm saying?"

"I think so."

"I like you, Olivia. I like you a lot. And I don't ever want to hurt you."

Her throat clogged at his heartfelt declaration. Men usually said they didn't want to hurt a woman right before they did exactly that.

"Olivia." He reached out and touched her face. "You're the first woman to capture my—" he cleared his throat "—*interest* since Sheila died."

Not exactly the opening she'd been waiting for, but she decided to go with it anyway. "Will you tell me about her? About Sheila?"

He settled back in his seat, closed his eyes a moment, then let out a quick puff of air. "She and I met in the third grade, one day after her family moved to town. The first time I asked her to marry me we were in the fifth grade."

Olivia drew in a couple of deep breaths. "That's really sweet."

"She was my first crush, my first kiss, my first everything, and she gave me two beautiful daughters that are my entire world."

The back of Olivia's eyes stung at the way his voice cracked as he made the declaration. Every part of her ached for him, from deep in her soul and beyond.

"But our marriage wasn't perfect."

"You just said she was your entire world."

Watching her from the other side of the car, he shook his head slowly. "That's not exactly what I said."

No?

"I loved Sheila. How could I not? We'd negotiated childhood together, grew into adults side by side. Our marriage was built on loyalty, trust and lifelong friendship."

Was it possible to love that deeply, for that long, and walk away from the loss without permanent wounds? "It sounds like you were very blessed."

"For the most part." He held her gaze for a long, tense moment, as if he were trying to tell her something without actually speaking the words. "Sheila and I got married right out of college. She had the twins three years later."

"You were still in medical school when they were born? That had to be difficult."

"Beyond difficult. I had zero free time. Sheila had to quit the job she loved to raise the girls. She wasn't happy about that, and eventually grew to resent me for it. Especially when we fell into our separate roles in the marriage and we—" he let out a slow exhale "—drifted apart."

The sound of regret in his voice had Olivia reaching out to cover his hand with hers.

"We lived in the same house, shared the same life, but we'd become strangers. I was so busy I didn't even notice until she gave me an ultimatum. She told me she'd given up everything to be my wife. It was time I got my priorities straight or give her a divorce."

Olivia gasped. He looked and sounded so stricken Olivia's breath snagged painfully in the back of her throat. "She couldn't have meant that. She was probably just trying to get your attention."

"Whatever her intent, it was the wake-up call I needed. We went into counseling. I learned to put my wife and daughters first, my medical practice second." He smiled distantly, his mind obviously lost in the past. "No regrets, either. My life has been richer for the changes I made back then."

Hard to believe possible, but Olivia admired Connor even more for the commitment he'd made to his wife and family. He'd done what was necessary to save his marriage and had no lingering resentment over that choice.

Not many people were capable of that kind of selflessness.

"Sheila and I were good again. Better than ever, and then she got sick."

The bitterness in his voice had Olivia gasping.

She'd heard about Sheila's ovarian cancer, but Olivia hadn't known the disease had been diagnosed after they'd worked through a rough patch in their marriage. Maybe no one knew. Maybe Connor had carried that burden alone.

"That had to come as a blow."

"We caught the cancer too late," he said, the words clipped but clear, and lacking all emotion. "There I was, a trained physician and I hadn't seen the signs, hadn't even known to look for them. She'd been tired, sluggish and had begun to lose her appetite. I chalked it up to raising twin toddlers."

"It was a logical conclusion."

Eyes blinking very slowly, his gaze unfocused, Connor flexed his fingers beneath Olivia's.

Olivia gripped his hand tighter.

"I should have insisted she get a checkup. I…" He shook his head and for the first time since beginning his story, his eyes took on an angry glint. "Her death was unnecessary."

His expression was unguarded, projecting an emotion she understood on a deep, personal level. Grief mixed with anger.

Olivia had suffered similarly when her parents died. And yet she didn't have the words to ease Connor's pain.

Maybe she wasn't supposed to give him words. Maybe grief that deep shouldn't be brushed aside with a handy speech.

Still, she felt compelled to say, "You can't second-guess yourself like this."

He continued speaking as if he hadn't heard her. "If I'd paid better attention, maybe I would have seen the physical changes in her for what they were."

The guilt in his voice touched a part of Olivia she didn't want to examine too closely right now.

This moment wasn't about her.

"Even if you'd have caught the cancer early, she still might have died."

"Perhaps." His voice was low and raw and Olivia knew her words had done nothing to help him.

Desperate to offer him the comfort he'd once given her, she chose her next words carefully. "I know this may sound empty to you right now, and you've probably heard it a million times, but God hasn't abandoned you. He's walking right beside you, waiting for you to turn to Him for healing."

Connor blinked at her, absorbing her words in silence.

She let him process them without interruption.

Words, no matter how logical or truthful, could only take Connor so far. The rest would be up to him. Only he could take the necessary steps toward making peace with himself and God.

As he lowered his head in thought, Olivia had a revelation. Connor's daughters weren't the only family members who needed her. Connor needed her, too.

And Olivia needed...

She didn't know what she needed. But she felt a sense of purpose growing inside her, a purpose that went beyond herself, beyond starting a new business, something powerful that included this man and his precious daughters.

Connor unbuckled his seat belt. "I'll pick you up in the morning, say seven-thirty?"

"That should work."

Saying nothing more, he exited the car but he took his time coming around to her side.

While she waited, Olivia gazed at her reflection in the passenger-side window. The image staring back at her looked determined, ready to fight for what she wanted.

Olivia wanted it all. Her own business where she got to call the shots. A man in her life to love with all her heart, a man who loved her with equal intensity. She wanted children, too, and a few dogs, maybe a cat and—

Her door opened and there Connor stood, hand outstretched, the streetlight wrapping him in its golden glow. She placed her palm in his and he helped her out of the car.

"Thanks for the ride."

"No problem." Hooking her arm through his, he escorted her up the walkway.

"You're walking me to me door?"

"What gave you the first clue? The walking part? Or my steering you in the direction of your house?"

She laughed. "You don't have to do this."

"I want to." He stopped, swallowed a few times, drew in a sharp breath. "I'm sorry I unloaded on you like that."

She hated that he regretted sharing his pain with her. "I'm honored you told me about your wife. Thank you for trusting me enough to share."

His lips curved in a smile and he leaned a little closer. "You're really something, Olivia."

He sounded a bit in awe. And maybe a little smitten.

Her pulse picked up speed. If he bent his head the slightest inch to the right, if Olivia shifted a bit to her left, and both leaned in a fraction more, their lips would meet.

Her heart did that strange stuttering thing it did whenever she was near this man.

She told herself to step back. Away from Connor.

She remained frozen in place, staring straight into those golden-amber eyes.

A heartbeat passed.

She took a very tiny pull of air and closed her eyes.

Was she really inviting Connor to kiss her, on her front doorstep, where anyone could watch them?

Someone was always watching in Village Green. Her eyes flew open.

Nervous again, she reached behind her, found the door handle at her back and twisted.

"Thanks, I..." She laughed self-consciously. "I'll see you in the morning."

"See you in the morning."

She scrambled into the house like a guilty teenager. She made it two full steps before she reminded herself she'd been raised with manners.

Stepping back outside, she closed the door behind her. Connor stood in the exact same spot as before. His eyes skimmed over her face. "Back so soon?"

She laughed. "Just so you know, I'm glad I came home when I did, glad I get to watch your daughters this summer."

He smiled.

"And I'm really glad we're..."

She wasn't sure how to say the rest.

A look of tender understanding filled his gaze. "I know, Olivia." He knuckled a curl off her cheek. "Me, too."

It was ridiculous how well he could read her. She looked away, gathered her thoughts, then forced her gaze back to his.

"I like you, Olivia." He smiled around the words, looking very much like the boy that had once instilled silly teenage hopes and dreams in her heart. "And I think we have something special growing between us. But before this goes any further, we have several things to discuss."

Boy, did they ever! "Agreed." She pumped up her smile. "But maybe we should give it a few days, think things through individually before we...talk."

He held her stare. "If that's what you want."

"It is." She needed time to gather her thoughts, to decide if she wanted to take a chance, to risk heartache again. She turned to go.

He caught her gently by the arm.

"Come here." He tugged her slowly to him.

Hope whispered through her. Connor was going to kiss her good-night.

But she needed to keep her head firmly planted in reality, needed to remember they'd only taken a small, tentative step toward each other. "Maybe we should..."

"Hush, Olivia." He touched his lips to hers.

She shut her eyes and told herself to stop thinking so hard, to enjoy the moment. A moment that ended all too quickly.

Connor stepped back. "See you tomorrow morning."

"Oh. Yeah. Okay." He was almost too attractive to look at this close up. "See you tomorrow."

He kissed her gently on the forehead and then was gone.

Speechless, fingertips pressed to her lips, she followed his progress down the walkway back to his SUV. She continued watching him as he climbed in the driver's seat with the long-legged agility that was all his own.

It wasn't until his taillights disappeared around the street corner that Olivia realized she was holding her breath. She let it out slowly. Very slowly.

And reentered her house in silence.

She had a lot to think about between now and when Connor picked her up in the morning. They'd crossed a line tonight. And now nothing would ever be the same between them.

Maybe that wasn't such a terrible thing.

Olivia predicted a long, sleepless night ahead of her. Nothing about her upcoming conversation with Connor was going to be easy.

Apparently, some things just weren't meant to be easy.

Chapter Fifteen

Connor didn't pick Olivia up the next morning. Avery did. And she wasn't alone. The twins were in the car with her. As was Samson, his stubby little tail wagging in a tight circle, his puppy face grinning from perked-up ear to perked-up ear.

Olivia settled in the front seat, greeted the girls, patted the dog on the head then looked over at Avery. "Where's Connor?"

Avery grimaced as she pulled away from the curb. "One of his elderly patients was rushed to the hospital early this morning. He wanted to check on her before he went in to the office." She gave Olivia an apologetic look. "He asked me if I could pick you up this morning."

The moment Avery finished her account of the morning's events, Olivia's phone vibrated in her purse. She pulled it out and checked the incoming text. It was from Connor. GOT HUNG UP AT THE HOSPITAL.

Despite the serious nature of his absence, Olivia felt a rush of pleasure, overwhelmingly pleased he'd bothered to text her at all, and a little surprised at her strong reaction to six small words on a cell phone screen.

But still…

Even in the midst of his concern for one of his patients, Connor had taken the time to let Olivia know where he was.

Olivia felt a sharp tug at her heart when a second text came through. REALLY WANTED TO SEE YOU THIS MORNING.

Again, she found herself unexpectedly moved and quickly thumbed her reply with unsteady hands. ME 2.

There was a brief moment of nothing. The girls whispered together in the backseat, heads bent over a handheld video game. Avery concentrated on the road. Samson bounced between the twins.

Olivia continued staring at her cell phone, willing Connor to reply. His answer finally came through, leaving her mildly breathless with anticipation.

SEE U TONIGHT AFTER WORK.

She took a risk and typed what was in her heart. CAN'T WAIT. Feeling especially bold, she sent another text with nothing more than a smiley face.

He responded in kind.

Uh-oh—her heart went *zing* again. As it had last night in Connor's SUV.

Sighing, she sat back in her seat and looked out

the passenger window. It wasn't supposed to be this way. She wasn't supposed to fall for Connor Mitchell. She had plans for her life, plans that would require every bit of her focus. Even if she didn't get the funding and had to take another job before opening her own tearoom, hadn't she learned her lesson with Warner?

Didn't she know the dangers of falling for another hardworking, single dad?

Then again, Connor wasn't anything like Warner.

He'd proven that on several occasions. More important, he seemed to value Olivia for herself, as the person she was. *Not* the person he wanted her to be, or even needed her to be so his life would go smoother.

What had started out as a temporary nanny position was fast becoming more. A situation full of a whole lot of…real.

Olivia was in trouble here.

Avery's throaty laugh cut through her growing panic. "Got something you want to share with the class, Miss Olivia?"

"No." Annoyance hiked her chin up a notch.

"Are you sure? Because you're looking awfully—"

"Still no." She stuffed her phone back in her purse, patently ignored Avery and swiveled around in her seat to address the girls. "Want to bake a chocolate layer cake this morning?"

Heads tilted at identical angles of interest, they answered as a single unit, "Yes!"

"You're making chocolate cake?" Avery groused. "I miss all the fun."

"We'll save a piece for you," Molly offered.

Avery shook her head. "I was hoping to lick the bowl."

"We can save you some icing. That's almost the same thing."

Still pouting, Avery turned onto Main Street. "I guess."

Olivia stifled a smile. But then inspiration struck as they approached the medical offices on the right side of the road. "Or we could make a special delivery later today."

Following the direction of Olivia's gaze, Avery sat up straighter in her seat. "Please tell me you're thinking of making that delivery to a certain medical office."

"Correct." Olivia tapped her nose with her index finger, then frowned. "Except…my car will be in the shop all day." She'd already called the garage this morning. The owner had agreed to pick up her car, but warned her not to expect it until later this afternoon. At the earliest. "No transportation. No field trip."

"No problem." Avery pulled into the parking lot of Connor's building. "Because you're going to drop me off at the office and come back this afternoon with a freshly baked chocolate layer cake, extra icing on the side."

Giving Olivia no time to argue, Avery practically

screeched to a stop, set the brake and hopped out of the car. She didn't bother looking back.

Laughing, Olivia moved into the driver's seat and smiled at the girls in the rearview mirror. "Let's go bake us a cake."

An hour later, after a side trip to the grocery store, Olivia decided two cakes were better than one. That way both girls could do equal the work, with the benefit of one for the house and one for the office.

Game plan set, Olivia put a large mixing bowl in front of each girl. "First, as with most cakes made from scratch, you'll need to cream the sugar and butter until the mixture is light and fluffy."

She showed them how. Then helped them measure and add the rest of the ingredients.

She showed them how to determine when the mixture was ready for baking. They then poured the liquid into cake pans, six in all, three per cake. Olivia put the pans in the ovens herself.

"Now, while the cakes cook, we'll work on the icing."

The twins waited patiently for her to guide them through the steps. Overwhelmed with affection, Olivia pulled them into a group hug.

You're in too deep, she thought. *Pull back before it's too late.*

It was already too late. Megan and Molly had become a part of her. Even if the Lord blessed her with more children in the future, these two would always be in her heart.

* * *

The moment Connor spied Olivia and the twins standing in the doorway of his office his heart tumbled in his chest. The picture they made personified family, a very loving family.

The girls, standing on either side of Olivia, looked happier than he'd seen them look in a long time. Maybe ever. Connor felt something move through him he hadn't experienced in years himself. Inner peace. The kind he wasn't sure he deserved, but wasn't foolish enough to dismiss.

"What's all this?" he asked in a hoarse voice.

"We come bearing gifts," Olivia declared, her eyes shining bright, as if she was having her own difficultly processing the moment.

Staring into that beautiful, mesmerizing gaze, Connor was tempted to pull her into his arms and kiss her as he'd done last night. How could anyone think she was a mere convenience?

Connor had never felt the urge to punch another man in his life. But now, when he thought about the pain and humiliation Olivia must have suffered from her ex-boyfriend's callousness, he thought about it. Thought about it real hard.

Swallowing back his rising agitation, he lowered his gaze, locking it on the cake in her hands. Be still his heart. "Is that chocolate cake?"

Megan beamed. "There's another one just like it at home."

"We made them all by ourselves," Molly told him. "Miss Olivia only helped a little."

Olivia. She'd done this. She'd put that look of pride on his daughters' faces. More than that, she'd turned a temporary nanny job into something... more. Something lasting.

Done in, Connor ran a hand down his face, drew in a hard breath. He thought briefly of praying, but he wasn't sure what he would lift up to the Lord. A prayer of thanksgiving for bringing this woman into his life, into his home, no matter how temporarily? A prayer for strength so he could remember Olivia had plans he couldn't ask her to give up for him and his daughters?

Or perhaps he was overthinking this. Maybe he should just let down his guard for a few precious minutes and enjoy time with his girls. All three of them.

"You like chocolate cake, don't you, Daddy?" Little worry lines dug between Molly's eyebrows.

"Who doesn't?" Even if he didn't, he wouldn't admit it now, not with his daughters' eager faces staring up at him and Olivia's encouraging smile warming his heart. He cleared his throat. "Let's bring it to the break room so the entire office can enjoy a piece."

Olivia's smile amped up a notch. "Lead the way."

Shouldering his way past them, Connor directed their small party down the hallway.

In that instant, if anyone asked him, he would

have said there was nowhere else he would rather be than right here, directing his daughters and Olivia to the break room. The thought brought a moment of peace, followed by a sudden wave of alarm.

A burning throb knotted in his throat.

Ever since Sheila's death, he'd been committed to creating a safe, healthy, happy home for his daughters. When he'd needed someone to care for them over the summer he'd done the logical thing. He'd hired a woman who met his initial requirements.

Yet today, as he watched Olivia set the cake on the table and begin cutting slices, he realized just how well she fit in his life, in his girls' lives.

They needed more than a woman's influence. They needed a woman's love. The unconditional, sacrificial kind that was described in the Bible, the kind that Olivia gave them without even trying.

Olivia Scott was an extraordinary woman. Her heart was pure, her compassion strong, her natural capacity to love vast.

She deserved a man who could give her the same level of devotion she would provide in return. She deserved a man who would give her his entire heart, and hold nothing back. A man who would make sacrifices for her and willingly rearrange his schedule without being given an ultimatum first.

His heart dipped, and a portion of his previous joy left him.

But then Molly threw her arms around him and

rested her tiny head against his chest. "I love you, Daddy," she whispered.

Overwhelmed with emotion, he pulled his daughter close and dropped a kiss on the top of her head.

She turned her face up to his. "Are you happy we came by today?"

He caught Olivia's eye. She gave him a quick, almost imperceptible wink. The intimate gesture sent his pulse beating in a fury.

"Very happy." Too choked up, he could say nothing more.

This didn't seem to bother his daughter. "That's good." She squirmed out of his hold and ran over to the doorway when Avery entered. "We brought lots of extra icing just for you."

"Fabulous."

Connor endured the next half hour with a smile on his face and a stoic resolve in his heart. No matter how hard he tried to enjoy the moment, his mind kept rounding back to one very important question: could he make a relationship with Olivia work?

Not without careful thought, a lot of planning and rearranging of his schedule plus a willingness on her part to do the same. It was a lot to ask a woman, especially one wanting to start her own business. One who might not even share Connor's feelings.

He thought she did, the suspicion confirmed when she looked up and smiled at him with the contents of her heart in her eyes.

In that moment, Connor knew what he had to do.

The thought had barely materialized when Ethan entered the room. "Cake!" He picked up a piece and immediately dug in.

Connor made his way to the side of the room where his partner stood. "I have something I want to discuss with you."

"Go ahead, I'm listening."

"Not here. In my office."

"Now?"

"Now."

Ethan snagged a second piece of cake and joined Connor in the hallway. "Is there a problem?"

Not if Connor had his way. "No. But I want to run something by you before I look into it further."

"Sounds ominous." Ethan settled in one of the two chairs facing Connor's desk, propped his feet up and dug into his second piece of cake. "Okay. Shoot."

Wasting no time, Connor got straight to the point. "I want to explore the possibility of bringing in another doctor to the practice."

Ethan chewed in silence. "Why now?"

A fair question. Connor closed his eyes. How did he tell his partner that everything had changed for him in a matter of months, making him desire a different future for himself? He yearned for things he'd convinced himself he didn't need, or particularly want.

A home full of love, with a good woman by his side, at least five kids and—go figure—a rowdy puppy or two.

"The honest answer is I want more free time with my family."

"You aren't getting enough?"

"I am. Now. But things may change in the future."

Ethan said nothing for a long moment. "This change in your future, does it have anything to do with my sister?"

Nothing got past the former Army Ranger. "Possibly."

"Dude, seriously? You're going to hedge? With me? About something as important as my sister?"

"I'm not hedging. I'm trying to—"

"Connor, stop. Stop talking. Before you dig yourself in a hole you can't get back out of." Ethan took another bit of cake, chewed in silence. "I've been wondering when we were going to have this conversation. I see the way you two are together."

Connor studied his friend for a beat. "I don't want to hurt her, Ethan."

"Then don't."

"It's not that simple. Let's say I'm trustworthy—"

"You are."

"You should be warning me away from her. It's the older brother thing to do."

"Why?" Ethan set down his cake on the desk, dropped his feet to the floor. "I've never known you to act dishonorably toward a woman."

That wasn't the problem. "My schedule is crazy."

"You made it work once before."

Connor nodded. He'd learned a hard lesson with Sheila. Did he want to do it again?

Ah, the million-dollar question. And the real reason he'd needed to talk with Ethan about his. He'd needed a sounding board he could trust. Connor also needed to make some serious decisions.

Ever since Sheila's death, he'd created a very specific day-to-day routine that hung by a fragile thread.

Sure, he'd been making noise about finding a wife, but he'd been thinking mostly in terms of the twins. Until Olivia had come home and reminded him there was more to life than just getting through the day. One step at a time.

Managing one crisis at a time.

Now Connor wanted more. He wanted it all. The whole happily-ever-after, riding-off-in-the-sunset dream come true.

Easier said than done.

Loving again, risking another terrible loss hadn't been in his plans. Nor was hurting a good woman he cared about. Maybe even loved.

If he were a praying man, now would be a good time to lift up a desperate request for the Lord's guidance.

Would God even hear him?

Chapter Sixteen

Life was never so good, Olivia mused, that it couldn't get even better. Though she and Connor had yet to talk about whatever it was growing between them, their relationship had definitely progressed beyond friendship. Nothing had really changed since she and the girls had brought chocolate cake to his office.

And yet everything felt...different.

Connor made it home on time nearly every night. He always called when there was an unexpected holdup, apologizing when and if he couldn't let Olivia know right away. He included her in every family activity, large and small, including the bedtime routine where they took turns reading to the girls.

Even with her mind—and heart—focused on Connor and his daughters, Olivia had found time to finish her business plan. Her next step would be to set up an appointment with a banker. Actually, she'd be wise to set up several appointments. Of course, it never hurt to have a personal connection. Olivia would ask Connor tonight for Hardy Bennett's number.

Since it was Wednesday, and that meant movie night in the Mitchell household, Olivia decided she would wait until the twins were in bed to broach the subject.

For now, while Connor set up the movie in the living room, she concentrated on creating her latest brainchild for her tearoom—chocolate-covered popcorn.

Her first batch was nearly complete.

As she spread out the popcorn evenly across the cookie sheet, Olivia couldn't explain why she wasn't more excited about meeting with a banker. She'd been planning this moment all summer, looking forward to it with anticipation. Yet here she was, dragging her feet, rather than jumping on the next step to make her lifelong dream come true.

Make a plan. Work the plan. Adjust when needed.

Where was the joy? The excitement?

Her hands paused over the popcorn. Why wasn't she working the plan with the same ferocity she'd applied to drawing up the proposal?

Because something had happened to her since she'd started, something life-altering. She'd met a single dad and his two adorable daughters. If Olivia worked her plan and eventually opened her own tearoom, that would mean she wouldn't be here, with

Connor and the girls every Wednesday night, watching a movie, laughing over Samson's latest antics.

Instead, she would be at her restaurant, serving her specially crafted creations to strangers, missing out on a treasured Mitchell family tradition.

Why, she wondered, as she drizzled gooey rich chocolate over the popcorn, did it have to be all or nothing? Why couldn't she apply the last part of her formula and simply adjust her plan?

Nothing was set in stone. No loan papers had been sighed, no building secured. There was time to rethink the particulars.

She could still call her own shots, be her own boss. So she wanted more. So she wanted both a family and a career.

She could have both, simultaneously.

Couldn't she?

She dripped the last of the chocolate over the popcorn and then brought the treat into the living room.

Connor and the girls were already settled on the couch, a large, comfortable sectional number that could easily hold another six people.

Olivia smiled at the picture they made. The three sat in their usual spots, the movie already started. The twins flanked their father but had left a space large enough for Olivia to squeeze in next to him.

She expected to feel nervous in his company. They still hadn't discussed their relationship. Nevertheless, she felt easy, relaxed, as if matters were settled in her mind and she could simply carry on with the rest of her life.

Wondering if he was as comfortable as she, Olivia plopped in her spot and glanced over at him. He was watching her with an unwavering gaze.

Her heart took an extra-hard beat.

There was something in his eyes tonight, something not altogether easy yet very, very appealing. Even without that "look" on his face, he was one fine male specimen. He'd changed out of his dress pants and polo shirt into a pair of cargo shorts and a black T-shirt that fit his torso perfectly.

No longer as comfortable as before, Olivia gave him a shaky smile. He winked at her.

Wow.

She could spend a lifetime looking into those smiling amber eyes with the thick, dark lashes. She leaned in a little closer.

A loud crash rent the air, followed by the sound of running puppy feet.

"Samson," Olivia and Connor said at the very moment the puppy launched himself over Baloo and landed smack in the middle of the couch.

Then plopped onto Olivia's lap.

The innocent-puppy expression fooled no one.

Molly quickly moved the animal to the floor and began a spur-of-the-moment wrestling match. Megan joined in.

Baloo ignored them all.

"You forget to put up the doggy gate?" Connor

asked, smiling fondly at the show going on beneath his feet.

"It would appear our boy has figured out an escape route." Shaking her head, she rose from the sofa. "I better go investigate."

"I'll come with you." Connor was on his feet a half second behind her.

As soon as they were around the corner, he pulled her to a stop. "I've been wanting a moment alone with you all night."

Flush with pleasure, she smiled up at him.

He pressed a kiss to her forehead, then stepped back and studied her face. "You look tired."

"Not especially. Lots on my mind, I guess."

"You don't have to stay for the rest of the movie."

"I want to stay."

"Has something upset you, Olivia?" He placed his hands on her shoulders. "Something you need to share with me?"

She remembered the finished business plan on her desk in the study back home. The one she'd spent months perfecting.

Where was her excitement?

Why this jolt of fear? This sense of foreboding that nothing was going to be the same after tonight?

She wasn't usually so pessimistic. Either she would get a loan for her business or she wouldn't.

She would either continue living in Village Green, working for herself, no safety net, no guarantees, or take a job in town until she could make her dream happen.

Either way, she would be her own boss. Eventually.

"I put the finishing touches on my business plan last night." Why did she sound so sad?

Misunderstanding her melancholy, Connor took her hands in his and squeezed gently. "Worried about the next step?"

The caring he demonstrated, as well as the understanding, only managed to make her feel sadder. Sighing, she nodded. "A little."

She wanted to take the risk, though. But what if it meant losing Connor and the girls?

No. *No.* The very idea made her breath come in quick, hard snatches.

In a move clearly meant to soothe, Connor pulled her close and smoothed his palm over her hair. "Want me to look over the proposal for you? I'm no banker and I don't know much about restaurants, but I know what it takes to run a successful business. I'm sure many elements are the same."

How...utterly...sweet.

"I appreciate the offer. But I'm confident the proposal is good to go. It's...time I made an appointment with a banker."

Connor eyed her closely. "Why the hesitation, Olivia?"

Truth. She should tell him the truth. "I'm afraid I won't get the loan. And I'm equally afraid that I will. Either way, my life will change dramatically. I'm not sure I'm ready for that."

He set her away from her. "The change could be for the good."

"It could."

"Make the appointment, Olivia." Connor placed a knuckle under her chin and lifted her gaze to meet his. "It's time to go for it. Besides, putting it off won't change the outcome."

"You're right." She held his stare, forced out a smile. "Do you have Hardy Bennett's number?"

"I do." He dug his cell phone out of a side pocket of his cargo shorts. "It's right here, in my contacts." He moved his thumb around on the screen. "I'll forward his information to you now."

She grabbed her purse off the foyer table, fished out her own phone and waited for his text to show up. When it buzzed through, she studied the screen. "Okay. Got it." She drew in a deep, steadying breath. "I'll call him first thing in the morning."

Connor moved a step closer to her, not too close but close enough for her to feel his silent support. "Wait until midmorning to call him."

Confused, she looked up from her phone. "Why?"

"I want to contact him first and let him know to expect your call."

The offer was so completely Connor. And again, really sweet. "You don't have to do that for me."

"It's often who you know as much as anything else in this town. You deserve every chance to make your dream come true." He smiled at her, a hint of sadness in his eyes. "If I can play a small part in that, then all the better."

She released a slow breath of air, and admitted the truth in her heart. She loved this man.

If only she knew what she was going to do about it.

Connor was going to lose Olivia. Maybe not today. Maybe not tomorrow. But he saw it in her face as she stared into his eyes. She was shell-shocked, upset and not at all happy.

He'd always known she was in his home on a temporary basis, but somewhere along the way he'd allowed himself to believe otherwise. To hope for something more, perhaps even a future together.

She's still going to be living in Village Green.

Even as the thought moved through his mind, another one followed on its heels. *Her time won't be her own for years to come.*

Who knew this better than him?

This was his chance to tell her how he felt, before she met with Hardy.

He kept his mouth pressed tightly closed. He couldn't—wouldn't—put her in a place to choose between him and her dream. Sheila had made that sacrifice; she'd given up her chance to chase her dream career and had grown to resent Connor for it.

Counseling had revealed her underlying anger that had festered over time. Even though she'd assured him she didn't regret having the girls, there had been a hint of sorrow that never quite went away.

Even after they'd restored their marriage.

In his head, Connor knew he wasn't responsible for Sheila's unhappiness. In his heart, he wasn't so sure. His career had always come first.

He wouldn't ruin another woman's dream, not even indirectly. "You're going to be a great restaurant owner, Olivia. You're an amazing, creative cook."

"Let's not get ahead of ourselves." She swiped her fingertips beneath her eyes, then squared her shoulders. "I'm only making an appointment to talk to a loan officer."

His heart already ached with a sense of loss. Nothing would be the same without her in his home. But change was coming.

The girls would survive. The puppy would survive.

Connor would, too.

Keep telling yourself that.

A crash sounded from the living room, followed by the inevitable "Samson, no."

A timely interruption. Connor took Olivia's hand. "Come on. Let's go see what that mutt's done now."

She gave him a shaky smile, then let him lead her back into the living room.

True to form, the puppy had upended a table. A very large table. "How can one small animal cause such chaos?" he wondered aloud.

"It's certainly a unique talent all his own." Olivia hoisted the dog into her arms while Connor righted the table.

"He didn't mean it," Molly said.

"He never does," Connor muttered under his breath, then noticed the movie credits were playing across the screen. "Time for bed." He took the puppy from Olivia. "That includes you, pal."

Samson licked his chin.

"Want Megan and me to take him outside?" Molly offered.

"I'll take him outside," Connor corrected. "While you and your sister get ready for bed."

"You'll let us say good-night to him, won't you?"

Connor shared a look with Olivia. "I always do. But right now you need to say good-night to Miss Olivia."

Both girls hugged her. She told them to sleep tight, don't let the bedbugs bite, then watched as they shuffled out of the room.

"Bedtime in twenty minutes," he called after them. "You can go on home, Olivia. I've got this."

"I'll clean up in here while you take Samson outside. Then I'll head out."

"Okay, thanks. Be right back."

As he marched the dog out the back door, Connor realized how much his life had changed since Olivia's arrival. Two months ago, he wouldn't have accepted her help so easily, no questions asked. She'd managed to move into his life and ease his burdens without him realizing it. She'd squirmed her way past his defenses and moved straight into his heart.

Ten minutes later, the dog was asleep in his crate and the girls were brushing their teeth. Connor took the opportunity to walk Olivia out to her car.

He reached to open her door, but she stopped him with a hand on his arm. "Connor, I want you to know, no matter what happens next, I plan to keep in touch with the girls." She looked up at the house, released a heavy sigh, then leaned back against her car door. "I want to be in their lives, any way I can."

The offer made him admire her all the more. "Does that offer include spending time with me, too?"

She answered without hesitation. "Absolutely."

"I don't want to lose you, Olivia."

Fat tears slid down her cheeks. "Oh, Connor."

He opened his arms and she launched herself at him. He caught her against his chest. They didn't speak, just stood there, holding on, both knowing things were about to change between them.

"Connor?"

He stared down into her face, saw the sadness. The hint of fear. And something else, something that mirrored the choke-hold clutching at his own heart. "Yeah?"

She smoothed the hair off his forehead, a gesture so full of care his throat ached from trying to keep it together. "I don't want to lose you, either."

He set her away from him. Maybe the changes

coming didn't have to be for the worse. Maybe they could be for the better. They wouldn't know unless they tried. "I have to attend the Village Green Hospital's annual gala Friday night. I was hoping you'd come along with me."

"You want me to go with you to the gala?"

"I do."

"Okay."

Was that a yes or an acknowledgment of his question? Asking a woman on a date was turning out to be harder than he remembered. Except...he hadn't actually asked her on a date.

He cleared his throat and tried again. "Olivia, will you go to the hospital gala with me? Will you be my date for the event?"

She stared at him a full ten seconds, which for the record was a very long time to wait for an answer.

"Yes, Connor, I would love to attend the gala with you." As she gave her answer, her guard dropped and he glimpsed the contents of her heart in her beautiful eyes.

She loved him. Olivia loved him.

A blessing he hadn't earned, and surely didn't deserve.

Momentarily overcome, he had to blink past the sting in his eyes. "I'll pick you up at six-thirty?"

"I'll be ready."

He reached for her, needing to say more, to assure her his heart was full of the same emotion that was in hers. But he stepped back and said nothing. The words wouldn't come.

Something deep inside kept him from declaring himself.

Wise? Or unwise?

Time would tell.

Chapter Seventeen

"I'm in love with Connor Mitchell." Olivia made this pronouncement to Keely in a whisper hidden behind her hand. She wanted to share what was in her heart before the other women in their Bible study showed up at the Turkey Roost.

Keely set down her cup of coffee and leaned back in her chair, her gaze never leaving Olivia's face. "So tell me something I don't already know."

"You...know?" Olivia all but gasped out the words. "But how?"

"Well, let's see." Keely wiggled her fingers in the air. "There's the way you look at him when you think no one's watching." She lowered one finger. "Not to mention the way your eyes light up whenever you talk about him." She lowered another. "And the way you manage to find him in a crowd, lock eyes with him and—"

Olivia held up her own hand to stop her friend

from continuing. "I get the picture. I'm terrible at hiding my feelings."

Keely laughed, her eyes twinkling with amusement. "If it makes you feel any better, he's just as obvious with his."

Only one to thing in response to that titillating comment. "Explain."

"He's as in love with you as you are with him."

"No, he's—"

"In. Love. With. You." Keely jabbed a finger in the air, aiming straight at Olivia.

"But...how can you tell?"

Up went Keely's splayed hand again. "There's the way he looks at you when no one's watching." She lowered one finger. "Not to mention the way his eyes light up whenever he talks about you." Down went another finger. "And the way he manages to find you in a crowd, lock eyes with you and..." She lowered her hand. "Do I need to continue?"

"No." *Yes*.

Olivia shut her eyes a moment.

Was Keely right?

Did Connor have feelings for her that went deeper than friendship and gratitude for taking care of his daughters? He treated her with respect and kindness and even encouraged her to go for her dream.

"When I told him about my appointment with Hardy Bennett at Village Green National Bank, he was supportive. Really supportive." Humiliatingly so.

"Yeah, I can see how that would make you think he doesn't care about you."

Olivia made a face at her friend. She treasured the fact that Connor understood why she wanted to chase after her dream, but she hadn't expected him to be quite so…encouraging. His response made her wonder if he wanted to get rid of her. "He said I shouldn't let anything stop me from opening my own tearoom."

"Again, not getting why that's so confusing to you. The man is not giving you mixed signals." Keely let out a wistful sigh. "It's obvious he cares enough about you to want to see you happy."

"I know. It's just…" She swirled her finger around the rim of her cup, a pang of disappointment clutching at her throat. "He didn't ask me not to open my own tearoom."

"Okay, now you've lost me." Keely leaned forward, hands flat on the table. "Why would he do that?"

"Because he couldn't bear to lose me? Because he knows how many hours it's going to take to make a go of it."

"Seriously?"

"His crazy schedule is hard enough to deal with. Add in me opening my own business and I have no idea how we'll ever find time to be together."

She looked down at her lap, baffled and confused and not sure what to think. Although Connor's support meant a lot to her, Olivia wanted him to make a stand. She wanted him to ask her to put family ahead of everything.

The way Sheila had?

Olivia sighed as wistfully as Keely had. Falling in love was real and it was hard and it was really, really complicated.

"Olivia, Olivia, Olivia. My dear, sweet, naive friend." Keely laughed. She actually laughed at her! "You can't really believe a man who loved you would ask you to sacrifice your dreams for him."

Warner had expected that of her. He hadn't used the specific words. But he'd made it clear he expected her to make his life easier. She was supposed to be there for him, his career and life more important than hers.

Olivia had told Connor this. Oh, goody, he'd been listening and taking notes. No wonder he was pushing her to pursue her dreams.

Not only because Olivia had told him about Warner, but because Sheila had given up her career to raise the twins and had come to resent Connor for it.

Olivia thought she might cry.

Pressing her fingertips to her eyes, she sighed heavily. How did she convince Connor she wasn't Sheila? And he wasn't Warner?

Eyes still shut, she tried to picture herself with him in her life.

"Olivia, you're getting all worked up before you even meet with the banker." Keely reached across the table and squeezed her hand. "Trust me, you don't want to make any decisions before you take that meeting."

Olivia opened her eyes, saw the look of sorrow in her friend's eyes.

"Decisions made quickly are always regretted later."

"I guess you're right."

"Of course I'm right." Keely planted her elbows on the table and rested her chin on top of her linked fingers. "Haven't you learned anything since you've been back in Village Green? I'm always right."

A masculine snort sounded a second before Ethan moved in behind Olivia. "In what lifetime are you always right?"

Keely dropped her hands to the table with a hard slap. "Nobody asked you, Dr. Scott."

Confused by the fierce scowl on her friend's face, Olivia swiveled her gaze to look up at her brother. A matching scowl etched deep grooves across his forehead.

"Ethan, what are you doing at the Turkey Roost at this hour?"

Had he heard her confession of love for Connor? Probably not. He barely acknowledged her. Keely, on the other hand, held his undivided attention.

Keely's scowl disappeared, morphing into a far-too-sweet smile. "You're staring, Dr. Scott."

He said nothing.

"And your sister just asked you a question," she

goaded. In Ethan's case, it was the equivalent of pulling a tiger's tail.

He tore his gaze away from Keely, the task appearing extremely difficult. Which seemed to make him even more tense.

Interesting.

"I'm picking up breakfast for the office." He spoke to Olivia, lifting a large to-go bag in his hand. "I came over to ask you what time your meeting at the bank is this afternoon."

"Two o'clock."

"I'd wish you luck but I read through your proposal. You don't need it." His voice held nothing but sincerity and brotherly admiration. "I know you'll do great."

He sounded sincere. "Thanks, Ethan. Your support means a lot."

He studied her face, looking as though he wanted to say more. But then the bell over the door jangled and one of the other women in their Bible study group entered the restaurant.

Olivia rolled her shoulders. Lacy Hargrove wasn't one of her favorite people, but the woman was honest about her flaws and openly admitted her soul needed work.

Who was Olivia to question her motives for joining their Bible study?

"Lacy." Olivia waved a hand in the air. "We're back here."

The woman wound her way through the tables.

Ethan's gaze took on a hunted look. "That's my cue to cut and run."

Before he turned to go he dropped a smile in Olivia's direction. "Let me know how the meeting goes. I'd really like to hear about it."

"I'll call you as soon as I'm finished."

"Good enough." He shot one last scowl in Keely's direction, then set out, taking a wide berth around Lacy.

Lightning quick, the woman changed directions and cornered him halfway through the restaurant. Hand clutching his arm, she leaned into him and said something.

He answered with a curt shake of his head, pulled his arm free and left the Turkey Roost without a single look back.

"Whoa." Keely blew out a slow breath, her eyes tracking his progress as he passed by outside the plate-glass window next to their table. "Who was that man and what did he do with your brother?"

Olivia had no idea. When she'd told him her idea for a tearoom in town, he hadn't scoffed. He'd asked tough questions, yet had asked them as he would an equal, treating her like a grown woman who could make her own decisions.

Who had he been talking to?

Connor, of course.

Olivia wasn't sure what to think about that. She didn't need the man to step in for her. She could fight her own battles. But, okay, admittedly, it was nice to know she didn't have to fight every one alone.

Lacy joined them at the table, greeting them cheerfully, her gaze lingering on Olivia. "I know this is probably inappropriate at a Bible study and all, but that brother of yours is one tall drink of water."

Keely snorted. "I can think of several other, far more accurate tags for the man. Bullheaded, stubborn and, my personal favorite, arrogant."

Lacy laughed, her features relaxing. "I take it you don't get along with Dr. Scott."

"Oh, he's fine. In small doses." She glanced over her shoulder, frowned at his retreating back. "*Very* small doses."

Her response seemed to satisfy Lacy.

Before Olivia could stop and wonder over either woman's reaction to her brother—opposite and yet somehow the same—the bell over the door jingled again. Two more women in their group stepped inside, the other two right behind them, with Avery bringing up the rear.

"The gang's all here," Keely said, straightening in her chair. "Let's order up some breakfast and dig into the Word."

Connor always enjoyed time off from the office, especially when that time included his two favorite daughters. As was their weekly habit, he took them to Hawkins Park. Samson was bored, according to

Molly, and needed another trip to the dog walk—
his third.

Megan supported this observation with an enthusiastic head bob.

Connor sent them on their way, with the requisite
warning "Keep him on his leash."

Although the weather was spectacular, the girls
both in excellent moods, something was missing.

Or rather, someone was missing.

Olivia. She'd been on his mind all day. He sat
down on the fountain's ledge and checked the time
on his cell phone, just shy of three. She should be
finishing up her meeting with Hardy at the bank.
Connor had wanted to call her beforehand, to give
her a personal word of encouragement, but he hadn't.
He didn't want to interfere in the process. She had
to make her decision on her own.

It was hard, Connor realized, trusting the un-
known. He didn't like feeling helpless. Total sur-
render was not in his nature, and no doubt explained
much of his current difficulty with the Lord.

Knowing Olivia had given Connor the desire to
work his way back to the Lord, to let go of his anger,
to trust God's greater plan for his life.

He hadn't called Olivia, but he'd sent her a text.

She'd texted back her thanks, or rather her
THANJXS. He smiled as he scrolled back to her text,
affection swirling through him as he reread the mis-
spelled word.

Assuming she'd turned off her phone during the

interview, he decided to send her another text so it would be there when she was through with the interview. CALL ME WHEN YOU'RE DONE WITH HARDY. I WANT TO HEAR HOW IT WENT.

Her response came immediately. ALREADY THRU. WALKING BACK TO CAR NOW.

Even if the meeting had started on time, it had lasted under an hour. THAT WAS FAST, he typed out.

MY PROPOSAL ROCKED!!!!!!!!!!!

Of that he had no doubt. He was happy for her. He was. But the sudden rush of longing made his eyes sting.

SO IT WENT WELL?

He waited for her answer, drumming his fingers on his thigh, throat tight.

Her response came a bit slower. HARDY LIKED WHAT HE SAW!!!! J J J J J

Connor's heart dipped, sorrow battling with the affection already there. He could hear Olivia's voice as she said the words, could see her give a little happy, heel-toe dance right there in the parking lot by her car.

He could continue seeing her, he told himself, dating her, giving their relationship a chance. The future didn't have to be an either/or scenario.

It would be difficult, though.

His time was already tight. Hers would be even more limited. Yet not trying wasn't an option. He'd spent four years barely feeling anything. Olivia had opened the floodgates. He couldn't return to the way things were before she'd come into his life.

The fact that he was considering a continuation of their relationship beyond the summer was a big step for him. And the girls. He needed to think things through, roll scenarios around in his head, analyze the various outcomes.

But first, he typed another message to Olivia. WILL CELEBRATE TONIGHT. At the last moment, he decided not to press the send button.

He hit the call button instead.

Olivia answered on the first ring.

"I take it congratulations are in order," he said into the speaker.

Her throaty laugh traveled through the phone, spreading warmth to the darkest edges of his soul. He loved her laugh. Loved her sense of humor.

He loved her.

He loved Olivia?

Of course he loved her. Still, the revelation would have knocked him to the ground if he hadn't already been sitting on the fountain's ledge.

"Although I appreciate the sentiment," she said through the phone. "Don't congratulate me yet." Her voice echoed in his ear, sounding as if she were in a tin room. An elevator, he guessed.

"Hardy say something to discourage you?"

"Actually, the opposite." She paused. "He thinks my idea is a good one. He even knows of a building coming open, a Mexican restaurant going out of business, that will be a perfect location for my tearoom. Right on Main Street."

"So that's good news, right?" He stood, felt the ground shift beneath his feet and quickly sat back down.

"It's great news, better than I expected." He thought he heard her sigh. "However..."

"What's wrong, Olivia?"

"I don't know. I have some reservations." She sighed again, this time the sound easy enough to discern. "It's all happening so fast. It's one thing to dream about something like this, another thing to make it happen. I need to bounce this off someone, talk it through, figure out what's what."

"I'm your man."

"Yeah?"

Oh, yeah. He tightened his grip on the phone, realizing how that sounded and, surprisingly, wanting to say it again. And again. And one more time for good measure.

He restrained himself. "I'm a good listener, Olivia, and an even better sounding board."

"You'd be willing to discuss the pros and cons, help me organize my thoughts?"

More than willing, he was eager to discuss the

particulars with her. "You better believe it. How about tonight?"

"Aren't you forgetting something?"

He felt his eyebrows pull together. "I don't think so."

"The hospital gala is tonight."

Perfect. "Those things are boring. We'll find a table in the back and... No, better yet, we'll make an appearance and then cut out early, right after dinner is served, and go somewhere where we can talk."

"I like that idea."

He did, too. But his phone beeped before he could tell her he agreed. Lowering the phone, he read the caller ID. "Gotta go, Olivia. The hospital is calling me."

"No problem. I'll see you tonight, Connor."

"Looking forward to it." He spoke over the buzz of the incoming call. "And, Olivia?"

"Yes?"

"The first dance is mine."

She laughed, the rich, husky sound full of unrestrained happiness. "Goes without saying."

Trying not to laugh himself, he switched calls with a smile on his heart and a slice of wonder in his soul.

He could get used to both sensations.

Chapter Eighteen

The knock came at precisely six-thirty. Olivia hurried into the foyer, intending to answer the door before Ethan or Ryder could.

No such luck.

Her brothers arrived in the tiny hallway at the same time as Olivia. Both were dressed in tuxedos, looking elegant and handsome, the kind of men that deserved a second glance. For a moment, she simply stared at them, feeling the full press of sisterly pride.

"Guess we're all going to the same event."

"Guess so." They grinned at her, looking like the boys from her childhood instead of the men they'd become.

Another knock came at the door. She waved off her brothers. "I've got this."

"No, Liv, we've got it." Ethan attempted to nudge past her.

She held her ground.

"Step back, Olivia." Ryder shifted her aside with

a hip bump. "It's our job as your older brothers to vet your date."

"Not even remotely funny." She shoved around them, a near-impossible feat since Ethan and Ryder were taking up all the room, elbowing each other to get to the door ahead of her.

Ethan's elbow connected with Olivia's ribs and she fell back a full step. "Ooof."

He reached out to steady her. "Sorry."

Ryder made his move for the door, smirking over his shoulder as he yanked it open. "Hello, Connor."

Olivia scowled at her brother.

"Ryder." Amusement in his gaze, Connor looked over his shoulder and connected his stare with Olivia's other brother. "Ethan."

The three men sized up one another, all but circling like a pack of dogs.

Olivia pushed her way through the tangle of testosterone.

"Ignore the prehistoric welcome committee." She looked pointedly at both brothers. "They were just leaving."

Ethan gave her the hairy eyeball. "Not yet, we aren't."

"Fine, then Connor and I are leaving." She linked her arm through his.

Connor remained frozen in place, his gaze locked on Ethan's. "I'll take good care of her."

"Yeah, you will." Ryder issued his own version

of the hairy eyeball. "And we'll hold you personally accountable if you don't."

"Understood."

A beat of silence passed. And then another. If Olivia didn't know better she'd think the three men were discussing more than just tonight's hospital event.

Ryder was the first to break ranks. "Now that we've got that settled, no driving fast or taking chances. You've got precious cargo with you."

Connor smiled down at her. "Yeah, I do."

At last, the Scott men stepped aside and let Olivia pass.

"Have a good time, kids," Ethan called after them.

"Not too good," Ryder corrected.

Already outside, Connor gave a single wave over his head, then opened the passenger door for Olivia. She waited until he joined her in the car before saying, "Sorry about that. They had no right to—"

"On the contrary." Connor took her hand. "They had every right. I'll be just as bad when the twins start dating."

"You're their father. Ethan and Ryder aren't mine."

"In many ways, Olivia, they are."

She thought about that, thought about all the times they'd come to her defense, stood in front of her, protected her from making a mistake.

She'd made mistakes anyway.

Yet now that she was back in Village Green, they'd been nothing but supportive, giving her space to figure out her next step in life without their interference.

"I should have come home sooner," she whispered.

Yet, if she had, she wouldn't have been so determined to set her own course, to reach for her dream. She definitely wouldn't have been in a position to help out Connor in his time of need.

God's blessing had shown up despite Olivia's mistakes. She was about to make her dream come true, not because of something she did but because the Lord had a better plan for her life than the one she'd been pursuing on her own.

Connor let go of her hand, put the car in gear and pressed on the gas. "The past is the past, Olivia. We all have to move on eventually."

Heart in her throat, she turned to look at him. "Does that mean you're no longer blaming yourself for your wife's death?"

"It means I'm coming to realize I can't control every part of my life. Either I can claw my way through the day, angry, holding on to the past and wondering 'what if' or…" He braked at a traffic light and turned to look at her. "I can trust there's a bigger plan than the one I can see. That everything happens for a reason."

As he spoke, his eyes communicated what he wasn't saying. That he was letting go of the past in ways he hadn't before. The significance of that stole her breath. Connor didn't sound bitter anymore.

Maybe a little resigned, weary even, but not as angry as the last time they'd had a similar conversation.

"Oh, Connor." She took his hand and pressed a kiss to the knuckles. "You're making me cry."

He frowned. "That wasn't the intent."

"They're happy tears."

He said nothing.

They arrived at Pinebrooke Country Club in silence, both lost in their own thoughts. Nosing his SUV into an empty space, Connor cut the engine and came around to her side of the car.

Outside the entrance, Connor tugged her to the side. "Take a walk with me."

Feeling suddenly vulnerable, and not sure why, she inched backward, shaking her head. "Connor—"

"Please."

The appeal in his eyes called to the part of her that could deny this man nothing. From the moment in Hawkins Park when their gazes had connected across the lush green lawn, Olivia had known her life would never be the same again. "All right."

Silently, carefully, she linked her fingers with his.

He drew her away from the entrance, then down a narrow sidewalk. As they walked side by side, Connor's nearness attacked the doubt clutching at her heart, making her believe, for one small second, that they could have a happy future together.

Hands clasped loosely together, they walked at a leisurely pace. Light spilled out of the country club, illuminating their path. The slender beam of the waning moon glowed small but bright, like the spark of hope in her heart. The farther they walked the more brilliantly the stars sparkled against the inky fabric of the sky.

Olivia reveled in the smooth camaraderie that fell between her and Connor. A comfortable serenity she thought might be what married couples experienced after years of knowing each other intimately.

They ambled past the main building. Only the stars and moon provided light now, the mountain standing guard in the distance as though protecting them against the fierce enemies of the world.

Connor looked to the heavens, took a deep breath then turned to face Olivia. "It's a beautiful night."

"Yes, very." *Now, Olivia. Tell him how you feel. It's the perfect time.*

She swallowed, losing her nerve as soon as she'd found it. Where did she start? For all their closeness, there were still moments like these that she felt slightly disconnected from him. As if he were holding a portion of himself back.

Or was that her?

Maybe Olivia was the one afraid to take a chance. Maybe she feared he wouldn't be able to love her as he'd once loved Sheila.

Well, of course he would never love her as he'd once loved Sheila. And that was all right.

Olivia didn't want to replace Connor's wife in his heart. She wanted to be what he needed now, to love him as the man he'd become.

Fearful she would blurt out her feelings, and botch he whole affair, Olivia started to turn back. His gentle touch to her arm stopped her.

For a split second, everything in her stopped.

Then…in one swift movement, he caught her against his chest. He dropped a kiss on the top of her head, the tender gesture breaking down the last of her defenses. This man had so much love to give. Did he know that about himself?

She pulled away so she could look him in the eye. His gaze softened, his eyes communicating something she couldn't quite name, didn't dare name. Just for tonight, neither of their pasts mattered.

Only now mattered.

This moment.

She rose onto the tips of her toes and pressed a kiss to his chin. "Connor—"

"Olivia—"

They laughed, then stepped apart. Olivia's heart rolled around in her chest, pounded violently against her ribs.

She would tell him she loved him. Tonight.

Connor took Olivia's hand and pulled her back to him. "Before we go in." He tugged her a fraction closer, determined to speak what was in his heart. "Thank you, Olivia. For coming into my life when you did, for showing me that barely making it through the day is no way to live."

"You've always done what's needed to be done,

Connor, and done it well. You've created a thriving family medical practice while raising two lovely daughters on your own."

"I've also made things harder on myself than they needed to be. Olivia." He took both her hands, willing her to him clearly. "I'm more balanced because of you. You've taught me how to share my burdens, how to rely on more than my own strength. Again, thank you."

"Oh, Connor." Her eyes shone like brilliant sapphires under in the moonlight. "You're the very best man I know."

"If that's true, it's because of knowing you."

He stepped back and stared down at her.

His breath hitched in her chest. Olivia stood gazing up at him, her heart in her eyes, her smile solely for him.

He took a moment to simply enjoy the view.

"What?" She touched her hair. "Something out of place?"

He closed the distance a bit more, touched her cheek. "If I haven't told you already, you look beautiful tonight."

And Connor was feeling especially tender toward her, more than ever before. The sensation made his heart pound so hard his chest hurt. Even Sheila hadn't made him feel like this.

He was coming to believe that was okay. He was a different man than one he'd been with Sheila. He wanted different things now, for different reasons. H only made sense he would want a different woman, *need* a different woman.

That didn't mean he would ever forget Sheila. She'd been there for all the firsts in his life. But it was time to let her go, once and for all.

"Thank you, Connor. You look especially handsome yourself."

They smiled at each other.

Things were getting very real. Everything was happening too fast. He had to remember his goals and desires for the future weren't the only ones requiring consideration.

Olivia's wants and needs were important, as well.

Connor took a step back, both mentally and physically. No matter how close he felt to Olivia at this moment, no matter how much he wanted her in his life, he had to let her reach for her dreams without him standing in her way.

He couldn't bear another woman he loved resenting him.

For Olivia's sake, he had to maintain perspective. "Tell me more about your meeting with Hardy."

"Not now. I want to enjoy the evening with you. No talk about the future."

Sounded good to him.

The inevitable was coming; he felt it, accepted it. But he would make the evening special for her anyway. And for himself, as well. He would ensure that this was a night they would both remember for the rest of their lives.

In silent agreement, they began the trek back to the country club. Two steps later, Connor drew to a stop again. "Before we go in, I want to do this...."

He pressed his lips to hers, gently at first, then with a bit more feeling before he stepped back. "Now we can go inside."

They decided to hit the silent auction before finding their table. If the crush of people was any indication, everyone in town had been invited to the gala. Connor wasn't sure how it happened, a jostle from the right, a shove from the left and he lost sight of Olivia.

He spent the next ten minutes searching for her dark hair among the sea of bobbing heads. Frustrated he couldn't find her, he made his way out into the hallway.

Still no Olivia.

He decided to head back into the silent auction but was stopped by a slap on his back. "Connor Mitchell. First on the phone and now in person."

"Hardy Bennett." Connor nodded to the banker, a man he'd known all his life. They'd even been on the same baseball team together in high school. "Wasn't expecting to see you here tonight."

"Tasha invited me, but I seem to have lost her in that madhouse." He hitched his chin toward the silent auction.

"My date's in there, too." Connor swept his gaze across the crowd, coming up empty again. "I figre if I wait out here I'll catch her when she finally makes it out."

"Not a bad idea. I'll wait with you."

They spent the next few minutes catching up on each other's lives.

When a lull fell over the conversation, Hardy said, "Hey, can't believe I didn't mention this sooner." He glanced at the doorway again. "But I want to thank you for sending Olivia Scott my way."

"No problem."

"That woman can write a business proposal like I've never seen."

Connor felt his shoulders bunch at the admiration he heard in the other man's voice.

"Of course." Hardy chuckled. "That's to be expected, given her background in corporate restructuring. She's dealt with far larger budgets than the one she presented to me this afternoon."

"So you were impressed with her idea."

"More than a little."

Although Connor wanted to ask Hardy specifics, the man continued talking without any prompting. "In fact, I'm thinking of renting her space in a building I own downtown."

"Olivia mentioned something about that." What she hadn't mentioned was Hardy owning the building in question.

"Did she?" Hardy shrugged this off. "The place used to be a Mexican restaurant, but they couldn't make a go of it with Señor O'Toole's as competition."

Connor felt a spike of dread. "You think a tea room will have a better chance?"

"Absolutely, especially with Miss Scott's idea to sell her chocolate creations as a separate operation from the tearoom business."

"So you think she can make a go of it?"

"Yeah, sure." Hardy nodded. "She has a solid plan in place. And since she isn't married and doesn't have kids, she'll have plenty of time to devote to the business."

The unspoken message was clear. Starting her own tearoom would require Olivia's undivided attention.

"I'm really looking forward to being a part of the process, even if all I do is rubber-stamp her loan application."

Connor tensed. Not wanting to know the answer to the question weaving through his brain, but unable able to resist asking it, he pressed for more. "Would you have considered giving her the loan if she'd had a husband and children?"

Hardy's face went immediately blank. "That would be discrimination."

"Right. Sorry I asked."

But he wasn't sorry, not for asking the question, at any rate. Despite his denial, Connor knew Hardy wouldn't be this enthusiastic over Olivia's venture if she was a married woman.

If that didn't just kill the evening for him.

Still, Connor knew what he had to do. He had to

break things off with Olivia. Something deep within his soul balked at the idea.

Tasha appeared in the doorway and Hardy straightened to his full height, ran a hand over his hair. "Ah, there's my date."

Connor forgotten, he took off toward the nurse, leaving Connor alone with his thoughts.

He shouldn't feel this disappointed, this let down over a woman that had only been temporarily in his life.

Nevertheless, the thought of saying goodbye to Olivia felt like a punch to the gut and a stab to the heart.

That didn't mean he wasn't going to let her go.

One woman had given up her dream to be with him, and had lived the rest of her life with regret. Connor would not condemn Olivia to the same fate.

Chapter Nineteen

To Olivia's way of thinking, the evening had been memorable, nearly perfect, one of the best in her life. Then came the moment when Connor settled into his SUV next to her.

With each mile they covered between the country club and her house, he grew more silent, more distant, almost cold. Olivia wrapped her arms around her waist, the gesture one of comfort and self-preservation.

Something had changed since they'd left the party. "Connor—"

"I spoke with Carlotta this afternoon."

The words were like a shock of cold water to the already icy atmosphere in the car.

Olivia tried her best to keep her voice even. "How is she doing?"

"She's ready to come back to work."

"Oh." She'd known this day was coming, but now that it was here she couldn't wrap her brain around the realization that she wouldn't be a part of the twins' daily lives. Or Connor's. "That's... good news."

"It is." His voice gave away nothing away.

Olivia dug her fingers into the fabric of her dress. This wasn't the way she'd expected the evening to end. She'd planned to tell Connor she loved him. That she was willing to do whatever it took to explore a relationship with him. But it would take both of them to make it work. And right now Connor didn't seem...invested.

"The girls will be glad to have her back."

"They'll miss you." He looked straight ahead as he spoke, concentrating on the road as if they were in the midst of a blizzard.

The weather was perfectly clear.

"Like I said before, I want to continue a relationship with the twins." She reached out to touch Connor's arm, pulled back before making contact. "And you."

He said nothing.

Not exactly full of words, was he?

Perhaps now was the time to tell him she loved him and wanted to try being with him.

But he pulled the car to a stop outside her house and turned to face her.

The sorrow in his eyes was a mere flash of emotion before he masked it behind a blank stare. "It's been a pleasure having you in my home, Olivia, caring for my daughters. And me. You've changed our lives for the better."

They why did she get the feeling he was about to say goodbye?

Dear Lord, no. Please, no.

"Oh, Connor, I love your daughters. I also lo—"

He exited the car, sufficiently cutting off the rest of her declaration. Opening her door, he waited for her to join him on the sidewalk.

When she did, they simply stared at each other. Connor had a look in his eyes, the kind a man got when he was about to make an important declaration.

But not a good one.

Again, he covered up his feelings with an unreadable expression. "Carlotta will be able to start back to work on Monday."

"I understand." She took his hand, clutched it tightly inside hers. "I want us to continue seeing each other, Connor, to explore what's growing between us."

It was the exact wrong thing to say.

"You're starting a business that will require every bit of your focus, Olivia. You know my crazy schedule." He cupped her face, his guard slipping enough for her to see inside his heart, to the vulnerable man who could love her as much as she loved him.

Why wouldn't he just say the words she desperately wanted to hear?

"There's something between us. I won't deny it.

And I think it could be really special. But it's not going to happen. We can't be together."

That was it? "Connor, no, please—"

He placed his lips on hers, a mere whisper of a touch, then pulled away.

She clutched at the lapels on his suit. "We can make it work between us."

Even as she said the words, she felt him pulling back, saw him put up an invisible wall between them. The one she hadn't seen in months.

"I know you mean that, Olivia, and we might even be able to sync our schedules for a while." He buried his face in her hair, breathed deeply. "But one day reality will set in. One of us will have to sacrifice more than the other, maybe more than we can bear. I won't let that be you, and it can't be me because I have two daughters to consider."

"It doesn't have to be all or nothing. One of us doesn't have to sacrifice more than the other. We can each make compromises. Fair ones that won't necessitate a need to feel resentful."

"It won't work."

She clung to him, desperation making her voice thick and raw sounding. "How can you know that if you won't even try?"

"Goodbye, Olivia."

She released him, swiped at her cheek. "That's it? You're quitting on us? Just like that?"

"We'll stay friends."

"You want us to stay…friends." She didn't want that. She wanted more, so much more.

"It's for the best." He placed another quick kiss on her lips. "I'll walk you to the door."

She held up a hand to stop his pursuit. "Don't bother."

She made a move to go, then stopped, took a deep pull of air and said, "Under the circumstances it might be better if I tell the girls goodbye without you there. I'll stop by Monday morning, after you've headed out to work."

He nodded.

She turned her back on him and opened the front door with her key. Not daring to look back, she walked inside the house and shut the door behind her with a determined click.

It was over between her and Connor, before it had truly begun. And she couldn't even pinpoint the moment when things had gone wrong.

Shattered, emotions raw, Connor simply stood outside Olivia's house, unmoving, looking at the shut door as though he could will it to open and Olivia to step back out.

The door remained firmly shut.

His chance to be with her was gone. And he couldn't help thinking he'd blown it. That he'd given up too soon.

"You look like you've lost your best friend."

Worse, it was so much worse. He'd lost the woman of his heart. "Go away, Ethan."

"I can't believe it." Ethan shook his head in utter amazement. "You cut her loose."

"It was the right thing to do."

"You sure about that?"

"I'm not in the mood for a discussion right now." He rounded on his friend. "Go away."

"Sorry, pal, but not a chance. I saw you with Olivia tonight. You looked happy, really happy."

Yeah, he'd been happier than he'd felt in years. But he'd let Olivia go anyway. For all the right reasons.

Then why did everything feel all wrong?

"It needs to be said, Connor, so I'm going to say it. You're connected to Olivia in a way you were never connected with—" Ethan cut off the rest of his words. "That is, you and Olivia are right together."

Connor closed off his emotions, and put the logical doctor in place, just as he'd done on the car ride here. "Doesn't matter." He continued staring at the shut door, willing Olivia to come back out, knowing she wouldn't. "It's over between us."

Ethan eyeballed him, his expression full of disappointment. "So you're really going to let her go."

"It's for the best." He pressed his lips into a grim line, the gesture mirroring the bleakness in his heart. "She deserves to reach for her dreams without me holding her back."

"Admittedly, I'm not much for giving advice in the relationship department—"

"Then don't."

"It seems to me you're not giving Olivia much of a choice in the matter."

"I'm not taking her choice away, I'm making it easier."

"On the contrary, you're stealing her decision."

"I'm putting her needs above my own."

Ethan snorted in disgust. "That's what you're telling yourself?"

"It's the truth."

"It's the coward's way out."

It took every ounce of Connor's strength not to react to the taunt. Ethan was wrong. His actions weren't cowardly. They were sacrificial.

And Connor was lying to himself.

His reasons for letting Olivia go were as much about him as they were her. He wanted her to succeed in reaching her dreams. But he also wanted to guard his heart from another aching loss, from enduring another marriage with a woman who resented him.

What if she doesn't end up resenting you? What if you can figure out a way to be with her without having her compromise her dream?

Needing to think in silence, without certain well-meaning friends breathing down his neck, Connor moved around Ethan. "Gotta go."

"That's it? You're walking away from my sister without a fight?"

"I'm not walking away. I'm heading home because I need to think."

"All right, then, while you're at it, think about this." Ethan came around to look him directly in the eye. "Olivia is an intelligent, gifted, caring woman who can make her own decisions. Let her."

"I'll take that under advisement."

"Connor—"

"Give it a rest, Ethan."

He made it home before eleven and found Avery asleep on the sofa. Not wanting to wake her, he went into the dining room and sat in the dark. He didn't know how long he sat there, letting the night's events soak in, before his eyes landed on the credenza.

Compelled, he walked over and opened the drawer that held the photo album of Sheila. He picked it up, noticed the Bible underneath and paused. He'd forgotten all about Sheila's Bible, having tucked it away years ago and not wanting to look at it since.

Now, hands shaking, he pulled it out, replaced the photo album and left the room. His footsteps heavier than before, he went into the kitchen, set the Bible on the counter and ran his finger over the worn cover.

In her last days of life, Sheila had found great comfort in the pages beneath his hand. Connor hadn't understood her need to have her Bible close, or why she'd felt bound to read from it even when her eyesight waned.

What was in there that had offered her such comfort?

Bracing himself, he flipped open the cover, shuffled through several pages, stopped when he came to a bookmark with a picture of a bald eagle and her favorite verse etched across the top. He set the slim piece of cardstock back in place, continued turning pages.

His hand froze over a pink envelope with Molly's and Megan's names scrawled on the front in Sheila's handwriting. She hadn't bothered to seal it.

Did Connor dare read what she had to say to their daughters?

What if it was something that would upset them?

What if it was something that would bring them peace?

He had to know. Before he presented the letter to the twins, he had to read what Sheila wrote first.

Throat burning, he pulled out the letter and began reading.

To my beautiful precious daughters,

I'm writing this with a heavy heart, knowing that I won't be able to watch you grow into adults. But I'll always be with you in spirit.

I'm sorry I'm leaving you without a mother. If I could stay, I would. But the Lord is calling me home now, and where I'm going there will be no more sorrow, no more pain, only joy and singing.

I pray one day your father will find another woman to love you as much as I do, who will treasure you as I do and will take care of you with kindness and grace. I pray she brings love into your home and teaches you all the things a mother is supposed to teach her daughters.

I grow tired, so very tired. But I want to leave you with one last thing. Raising you two girls was the joy of my life. If I had it to do all over again, I would make the same decisions. Tell your father I love him, have always loved him and stop being so hard on himself. I can't wait to see you in heaven one day. I love you always,
Mom

Connor's eyes filled with tears and his heart clenched hard in his chest. He recognized the gift he'd just been given, one he hadn't been expecting, and would share with his daughters when they were a little bit older.

Sheila hadn't resented him. She hadn't regretted giving up her career to raise her daughters. She wanted him to move on with his life, to provide a happy home for himself and their daughters.

A wave of peace passed through him, the sensation soft and healing and dragging the tears out of his eyes.

With mechanical movements, he refolded the letter and stuffed it back inside the envelope. He placed both against his heart and said the words he'd never been able to say until now.

"Goodbye, Sheila."

Chapter Twenty

Make a plan. Work the plan. Adjust when necessary.

The winning formula had already brought Olivia further than she could have imagined a few months ago, allowing her to turn a lifelong dream into a full-blown reality. She would be wise to continue relying on those same three steps for other areas of her life.

Thus, she made her next plan, the most important of her life.

Step One. Give Connor the entire weekend to come to his senses and not a day more. By Monday morning, if he hadn't sought her out first, then Olivia would take matters into her own hands and go to him herself, explain all the reasons why they belonged together.

It was a good plan.

A workable plan.

No adjustments necessary.

Fortified with her new strategy in mind, she

plucked her keys out of her purse and headed out to meet Keely at the church.

Hand on the doorknob, she experienced a moment of overwhelming panic. What if she couldn't convince Connor to take a chance on her, on them?

No. She wouldn't give in to doubt. Doubt had no place in her plan.

Olivia simply needed to practice what she would say to Connor. Not that she hadn't already done that, all day yesterday and last night. In fact, maybe she wouldn't wait until tomorrow morning to speak with him. Maybe she would head over to his house now and—

"Connor?"

"Hello, Olivia."

There he stood, on her front doorstep, looking at her in a way that made her knees threaten to give way. His handsome, heart-stopping face showed signs of stress, especially around the eyes, but she saw something else in his gaze, as well.

Something sweet and maybe a little vulnerable. Something that looked a lot like love.

He studied her face as if he'd been hungry for the sight of her. She liked being the center of all that masculine attention.

Then he smiled.

And her heart sighed.

Right then, in that precise moment, Olivia knew everything was going to be okay between them.

She closed the distance, conscious of his solid

strength as she approached him, as well as her need for him in her life. She wouldn't let him leave until she made that abundantly clear.

"I have a lot to say to you," he said softly, breaking the silence first.

So much she wanted to say to him, too. But everything in her heart came down to three simple words. "I love you, Connor."

"I love you, too, Olivia."

He'd said the words. He'd finally said the words. They were going to be okay.

Forcing his gaze free of hers, he took several bracing breaths and then turned back to her. "I'm sorry, Olivia. I made a decision about our future without giving you a chance to share in the process."

"Yes, you did."

"I need to tell you why."

Although he'd made his reasons clear enough the other night, she nodded. "All right."

He guided her to a bench beneath a tree in the front yard, waited for her to sit before joining her. "You already know Sheila got pregnant with the girls while I was still in medical school."

"Yes." Olivia touched his hand in a show of comfort. "And she had to quit her job to raise the girls."

"Neither of us was prepared for the demands that came with caring for two infants." He rubbed a hand over his face. "We were young and naive and convinced she would be able to go back to work in six weeks, maybe two months."

He paused, but not long enough for Olivia to say anything in response.

"Sheila wasn't happy about giving up her career, but she did it. For me. For the girls. Because of things she said in counseling, I assumed she resented me for that. I now know the truth. I was wrong."

He seemed certain, and looked as if a weight had left his heart, as if a heavy burden had been lifted. "What convinced you otherwise?"

"I found a letter she left for the girls. The specific words are meant for them, alone." He glanced at a spot over Olivia's shoulder. "But I can tell you her greatest joy was being their mother."

"Oh, Connor." Olivia closed her hand over his. "I'm so glad to hear that. For the girls' sake. And for yours."

"I made a decision about us, based on what happened with Sheila. That wasn't fair to Sheila. And it definitely wasn't fair to you." He pulled her hand to his lips. "Forgive me?"

"Of course I forgive you."

"I want to be with you, Olivia. More than that. I want to do the work to be with you, whatever it takes. I want to figure out a way to sync our schedules."

"I like the sound of that."

"Your time will be tight as you focus on your business. That's why I'm thinking of freeing up some of my time."

The sound of her heartbeat thundered in her ears. "You'd do that for me?"

"Yes, Olivia." He held her stare. "It'll be easier if Ethan and I bring in a third partner to the practice. In fact, I've already broached the subject with your brother."

"You...you have?"

"I want to be with you, Olivia. I want time with both you and the girls."

Overcome with love for this generous man, eyes burning, she curled her fingers around his. "You know I love Molly and Megan nearly as much as I love you."

He took her hand and pressed his lips to her knuckles. "They love you, too, nearly as much as I do."

"Oh, Connor." His name came out sounding raw, almost strangled, and then the unthinkable happened. Tears spilled down her face.

"Don't cry." He wiped his thumb across her cheeks. "Please don't cry. You're going to do me in before I can say everything I came here to say."

"I'm sorry, I just..." She attempted to laugh through her tears. "Go on."

"The man you met in Hawkins Park was sleep-walking through life, often collapsing in bed at night, only to do it all over again the next day."

Smiling through her tears, she said, "That takes remarkable internal strength and is one of the many things I admire most about you."

He rolled his shoulders. "I was barely getting by on my own. That was easier than dealing with my grief and moving on with my life."

"Perfectly understandable, you'd suffered a terrible loss."

"I might have spent the rest of my life secreting my anger away until it destroyed me. But then you came along. You helped me take the first steps toward healing. And now I'm blessed beyond measure. I have my family, my precious daughters and—"

"You also have me."

"I also have you." He shifted, repositioning his legs so that he could lower to one knee in front of her. "I want you in my life, Olivia, always. I want to stand by your side in good times and bad. I want to share your burdens, and allow you to share in mine. I'll be your strength when you think you can't make it another day and—"

"I'll be *your* strength when you think you can't make it another day."

"Olivia Marie Scott." He took her hand in his, brought it to his lips. "I can't promise you a perfect life. There's no telling how many days any of us have left. But I want to spend every one of them with you. Will you marry me?"

"Yes." She kissed him squarely on the lips. "Yes, Connor, I'll marry you. I'll be your wife for the next seventy years, seven days, or however long the Lord ordains."

"I like the sound of that." He pulled her to her

feet, wrapped his arms around her and held on tight. "Let's go home and tell the girls we're getting married."

As far as Olivia was concerned, it was the perfect beginning to the rest of their lives together.

Epilogue

Olivia hoped years later, when the twins were adults and planning their own weddings, they would look back on this day with fondness. Not only was it the day the four of them officially became a family, but it was the day Olivia became their mother.

The event had come together seamlessly, thanks to the girls' invaluable input and the welcome assistance of Avery and Keely.

Now, with all the preparations complete and the guests in their seats, Olivia stood beneath a trellis in the backyard of Charity House, and recited her vows to the man standing by her side. "I can't imagine a day without you in it or my life without you there to share the ups and downs with me. You are a part of me, joined to my soul as well as my heart. I love you, Connor Mitchell, and promise to keep on loving you for the rest of my life."

She turned to address Molly and Megan, who were standing beside her in their role as her maids of honor. "No matter how many children the Lord blesses me with in the future, I won't love them any more than I love you two." She pulled them against her, uncaring that the gesture crushed her dress. "You are the daughters of my heart."

Eyes shining, Connor took his turn reciting his vows. "Olivia. I've lived a blessed life and, eight years ago, was given the added joy of two beautiful daughters. That's more than any man can hope for in this life."

The girls beamed up at him.

"But the Lord wasn't through showering His blessings on me. He brought you into my life. You are my present and my future." He squeezed her hand. "I love you, Olivia Marie Scott, and promise to love you for the rest of my life."

The pastor nodded, smiled at each of them, then took a moment to impart a bit of wisdom. "We live in world full of distractions. The busyness of life can be a source of great conflict in a marriage. Loving compromise will be required of you both, and a willingness to sacrifice on each other's behalf a necessity for a happy life together."

Olivia shared a meaningful look with Connor. The day after he'd proposed, she'd signed the loan papers for her tearoom. Construction was nearly complete, her menu set and she would soon be opening her doors to the public.

Connor had been supportive every step of the

way, and was down to the last two candidates in
his search for another doctor to add to his practice.

Oh, how she adored this man.

He looked especially handsome in his tuxedo.
A shiver of anticipation traveled up her spine. The
ceremony was almost complete. She was moments
away from becoming Connor's wife.

As her groom slid a beautiful diamond ring on her
finger, Olivia cast a glance at the girls next to her.

Her girls. Her daughters.

Another member of their family caught her eye.
Sitting at Connor's feet was a very handsome, very
well-behaved Samson. He only broke form with a
loud bark when the pastor said, "I now pronounce
you husband and wife."

Connor pulled Olivia into his arms and kissed her
soundly on the mouth. "I love you, Mrs. Mitchell."

She smiled into his golden-amber eyes, rose on
her toes and kissed him right back. "I love you
more."

"Not possible." His arms slid around her and he
went in for another kiss.

Molly cleared her throat and they laughingly
broke apart.

Arm in arm, they began their walk back down
the makeshift aisle between the chairs the caterers
had lined up for the occasion.

Molly and Megan followed closely behind.

Sitting in the front row, Avery winked at Olivia.
She returned the gesture, realizing she had a sis-

ter now. No, she had *four* sisters. Plus two daughters. And, of course, a handsome, attentive husband.

Olivia sighed happily.

Connor continued guiding her down the aisle. Each step pulled her away from her past and closer toward her future, the one she would share with this man and his daughters.

She turned her face to Connor.

He planted a tender kiss on her nose. "I have a gorgeous wife." He tucked a strand of hair behind her ear. "And two beautiful daughters." He reached out and pulled the girls in close. "And, I can't believe I'm saying this, a well-behaved dog to complete our happy family."

Proving his point, Samson trotted up to them and obediently plopped his behind on the ground when Olivia said, "Sit."

"Well-behaved dogs are so boring," Molly declared, executing an impressive eye-roll she'd picked up from her aunt Avery.

Olivia laughed at her scowling daughter.

"You know how much I love you, right?" She moved her gaze from Molly to Megan, then over to Connor. "All three of you?"

"Good thing, too." Connor kissed her on the lips. "Because you're stuck with us for the rest of your life."

Only one thing to say to that. "Praise the Lord."

* * * * *

Dear Reader,

Thank you for choosing *Claiming the Doctor's Heart*. This book was especially fun for me to write because I had the chance to explore several of my favorite romance novel themes: widowed single parents, twins, family, small towns and, of course, unruly puppies creating mayhem.

Each of these themes has touched my life personally. I have a twin sister. I'm married to a former single parent. I come from a large family, grew up in a small town and always had a dog or two running wild in the house.

The medical profession is especially dear to my heart. Many of my family members work in the health-care field. Most are doctors; others are nurses, while some are researchers making strides against deadly diseases.

This book honors their hard work and dedication. Though mealtimes often included at least one empty seat at the table, I learned when people's lives are at stake sacrifices must be made. A late-night dessert with my father was always worth the wait, even if that meant eating cake at midnight.

I love hearing from readers. Please feel free to

contact me at my website www.reneeryan.com. You can also find me on Facebook or Twitter.

In the meantime, Happy Reading!

Renee

Questions for Discussion

1. What event drove Olivia back to her hometown? Have you ever been in a situation that made you reevaluate your life? What did you do?

2. Who does Olivia meet in Hawkins Park? What is her connection to this family, if any? How does this meeting end?

3. What does Connor's housekeeper Carlotta's injury mean for him and his family? Who comes to his rescue? Have you ever been in a situation that left you desperate to find an immediate solution, if not the best solution? What was the result?

4. Why is Connor shell-shocked when he comes home and finds Olivia in his kitchen? How does Olivia handle the situation? Would you have handled it differently? If so, how?

5. What happened to Connor's wife? Why does the way she died, not to mention the timing, cause him great pain, guilt and feelings of helplessness? What has his life been like since she died? How have his priorities changed?

6. What has life been like for Molly and Megan since their mother died? Why do they continually introduce women to their father?

7. The twins fall ill the day after the baseball game. Does Olivia's assistance help or hinder the situation? How does Connor react to her assistance? Is this the same way he would have reacted a month ago? Why or why not?

8. Why does Connor forgo attending church? Despite his avoidance, why do you think he hosts Sunday dinners at his house? Do you think this shows he's on the road to healing? Why or why not?

9. What does Avery tell Olivia to do about her relationship with Connor? How does Olivia respond?

10. How does Connor help Olivia reach her dream of opening her own tearoom? Why is helping her important to him? What risks are involved for him, personally?

11. What changes Connor's mind about breaking up with Olivia? Does he finally achieve closure over his wife's death? If so, how? What

does he say to Olivia when he comes to her after going through his wife's Bible? How does Olivia respond?